W9-AUI-204

Carnage at Christhaven

CARNAGE AT CHRISTHAVEN

A SERIAL MYSTERY NOVEL

by certain members of
The Chrysostom Society

edited by
William Griffin

Harper & Row, Publishers, San Francisco

New York, Grand Rapids, Philadelphia, St. Louis
London, Sydney, Tokyo

 For information address Harper & Row, Publishers, Inc., 10 East 53rd Street, New York, NY 10022.
FIRST EDITION

Library of Congress Cataloging-in-Publication Data

Carnage at Christhaven : a novel / the Chrysostom Society.—1st ed.
p. cm.
Contents: Eschaton à la carte / by William Griffin—Without one plea / by Robert Siegel—The shepherd who came in from the cold / by Walter Wangerin, Jr.—Night of the living dead / by Stephen R. Lawhead—The pool / by Madeleine L'Engle—In the women's room / by Karen Burton Mains—The blue tattoo / by Calvin Miller—Nothing good ever comes / by Alice Slaikeu Lawhead—Kyrie, eleison / by Richard J. Foster—Avenge, O Lord, thy slaughtered saints / by Emilie Griffin—The muse is much amused / by Luci Shaw—Mysterious ways / by Harold Fickett.
ISBN 0-06-061379-3 : $9.95
I. Chrysostom Society.
PS3550. A1C37 1989
813′.54—dc19 88-45998
CIP

---

89 90 91 92 93 BANTA 10 9 8 7 6 5 4 3 2 1

CONTENTS

PREFACE

Whether one is a Mafia chieftain or a Christian scrivener, mountaintops seem to be the place to go for epiphanies, transfigurations, and strategy planning sessions.

On October 20, 1986, the writers Steve Lawhead (*The Search for Fierra* and *The Siege of Dome*), Walter Wangerin, Jr. (*The Book of the Dun Cow* and *Orphean Passages*), and Philip Yancey (*Fearfully and Wonderfully Made* and *Where Is God When It Hurts*), flew to Colorado Springs, where they were motored fifty miles to a rustic lodge in the Rockies.

Richard J. Foster (*Celebration of Discipline* and *Money, Sex & Power*) was the summoner; he was associate professor of theology and writer-in-residence at Friends University, Wichita. Aiding him in the summoning were Calvin Miller, a Baptist pastor from Omaha and author of twenty-three books, and Karen Burton Mains, author of nine books, some of which she had coauthored with her husband, director of the national radio broadcast "Chapel of the Air."

Because of Mains's industriousness, what began as an authors' conference and developed into an authors' retreat was funded by Charles "Kip" Jordon of Word, Inc. "Serious literary and academic writers provide the seed for the popular writings of the next generation," said Jordon at the meeting. The choice of authors invited to the meeting he had left to Foster, Miller, and Mains; only one of them had been published by Word.

Foster's intention, announced in a letter sent out the previous April, was "to consider the feasibility of establishing a National Guild of Professional Writers," whose literary efforts flowed out of a Christian worldview. And he and the other eleven writers—whose works had collectively sold perhaps five million copies—began talking in front of a roaring fireplace on the night of the twentieth. They soon found that it was about as possible to kick about a Christian *Weltanschauung* as to put the boot to a leathern earth ball.

The concept of the guild was not at all appealing to Madeleine L'Engle, whose *Swiftly Tilting Planet* and *Wrinkle in Time* are read around the world. She and some others proposed that the group should be as informal as the Inklings, the legendary writers' group that included, among others, C. S. Lewis and J. R. R. Tolkien; that its membership should be limited to some but not all Christian writers; and that twenty should be the optimum number of such members.

As the idea of such a guild went smoking and whistling up the chimney, the conversation turned toward other ways in which the Christian writers could make their presence felt in the generally unappreciative world of American letters. Writers of quality themselves, most felt debauched by the recent Christianized versions of Mother Goose and Robert Louis Stevenson—books that were the products of hyperactive, if Christian, imaginations. Most energetic was the proposal of a Christian version of the *New York Review of Books,* made by Harold Fickett, novelist and short story writer whose most recent work was *Flannery O'Connor: Images of Grace.*

Oddest proposal of the two-day meeting was made by the least of the group. I, whose only major work was *Clive Staples Lewis: A Dramatic Life*, suggested that the members write a murder mystery in which each would contribute a chapter. This would be not unlike *The Floating Admiral,* one of four serial mysteries published with éclat some decades ago by such members of the Detection Club as G. K. Chesterton,

Dorothy L. Sayers, Ronald A. Knox, Clemence Dane, and Agatha Christie.

I half expected responses like "How imaginative!" and "I feel sorry for his wife!" and "Don't think twice about him—he's from Vatican City!" L'Engle, however, responded instantly and, I assumed, affirmatively. Robert Siegel, a poet of some stature and author of *Whalesong* and *Alpha Centauri,* whispered what I thought was his willingness. Luci Shaw, a poet of not a little accomplishment and president of her own publishing house, just looked willing.

Someone suggested as a working title *Carnage at Christhaven.* It engendered a certain amount of jollity, which I later came to interpret as a subtle agreement—it was the only agreement of the two-day affair—not to oppose the project in public. My wife, Emilie, author of *Turning: The Experience of Conversion* and *Clinging: The Experience of Prayer,* simply put her hands over her eyes and endured.

Well, I wrote the first chapter, and ten of the other eleven writers present that October in the rock-bound, snow-swept lodge, probably against their better judgment, contributed the successive chapters. Matthias to the group was Alice Slaikeu Lawhead (*The Christmas Book* and *Voices*), who made the group a perfect twelve again.

As the mystery novel turned out, the group, which by its second meeting had expanded and become known as the Chrysostom Society, not only wrote the chapters but are themselves the remote inspirations for most of the characters in the work. As I chose to accentuate the eccentricities of my fellow writers, so they focused on mine and soon on each other's. The result we would like to think is, if not the perfect murder mystery, then at least an acceptable comedy of religious manners in the 1980s.

Success, if the work should enjoy that, is due to the eleven who chose, possibly risking their professional reputations, to contribute a chapter. Failure, if the work should suffer that, can be traced only to me, who had the temerity to suggest the idea in the first place and indeed had nothing to lose in the process.

William Griffin
New Orleans
April 1, 1989

Carnage at Christhaven

Gullible readers, beware! *Carnage at Christhaven* is a work of fiction and parody whose intention is to amuse, not to instruct. As such, it is the product of the collective imagination of the authors about a world that doesn't, to the best of our knowledge, exist.

THE AUTHORS

Chapter 1

ESCHATON À LA CARTE

WILLIAM GRIFFIN

To the mountaintop they had come as if on pilgrimage. To the upper room they had climbed as if for fellowship. To Christhaven, a lodge in the Colorado Rockies, the twelve members of the All Hallows Society had wended, Christian writers whose published works—if the *New York Times Book Review* had fingers enough to count—sold in the millions.

Winded, for the site was many thousands of feet above sea level, they had been summoned by George Gloster, a pastor and professor of friendly persuasion. For some time now he had a vision that if Christian writers who wrote and published singly assembled collectively, they might attempt something mighty for the Lord. "What do you think of the Christian Mother Goose?" was the critical question he had put to his guests over the long lines when inviting them. "Not much," was the answer he expected. When asked in return, he managed to reply, "About as much as I do of Scripture Cookies and Scripture Tea."

As the cocktail hour approached, the guests assembled in the flagstone lobby, not to have cocktails, for alcohol and nicotine were forbidden substances on Christhaven property, but to be welcomed by Gloster and to be introduced to the other guests.

"What is this all about?" demanded Philippa d'Esprit, an elderly Episcopalian, a prolific writer of adult stories for children. Erect, bejeweled, gowned in brocade, she might have been a Borgia or even a Sitwell; planted in a wing chair on the red carpet, she might well have been flanked by porcelain greyhounds, sitting for a portrait by Tchelitchew. "I belong to enough groups already."

"After dinner, that's a dear," said Gloster, "we're going to meet around the fireplace."

"I hope that doesn't mean that we're going to *share!*"

Dark outside, the lobby was lit by a circular, wagon wheel chandelier hanging from the ceiling. Such warm air as was in the enormous room rose to the rafters, only to be wafted downward by wooden-bladed fans circulating at slow speed.

"You look older than your dust jacket photographs," said Harold Hastings, dipping a tentative toe into the conversation.

"I'm so old," said d'Esprit in warm sepia tones, "that I knew your father."

"But that isn't old. He died last year."

"I knew him in the eleventh century," she said, wrinkling back in time. "He was a knight inhospitaler, which means that he was mean to the Christians when they were being mean to the Muslims. I think you take after him."

"So you're not old," said Hastings, trying to tread water. "You're only middle-aged."

"I bet I can do more laps than you," she charged, her bony fingers pointing like trident tines to the swimming pool, which lay behind thermal floor-to-ceiling windows on one wall of the lobby.

"I don't swim," said Hastings, avoiding a Poseidon adventure of his very own.

"I didn't want to come," said Livingston Johns, a collegial teddy bear in brown corduroy suit, with two fantasies and two books of poetry under his belt with the Lord of the Rings buckle. "But I had to come if only to hear what everybody else is going to say about me."

"You could have stayed at home," said Hastings; "*I've* never heard of you."

"I only wish I hadn't heard of *you*," said Johns, returning the compliment.

"Testy, testy, testy," said Gloster. "Let's not be testy."

"But it's snowing outside!" Hastings was eating an Eskimo Pie bought at the front desk for half a dollar.

"And it looks as though it's not going to stop for the next forty-eight hours," said Gloster. "I hope you brought your skis. Generic skis, of course; not brand-name ones," he said with a grin, harking back to a recurrent theme in several of his books on spiritual discipline. "That would be not only ostentatious but also expensive, money that could better be used elsewhere."

"I don't ski, and what's more, I hate it when it snows," said Hastings, flinging himself down on a sofa. There was an unholy noise, and he bounded up again. Lifting the cushion, he fully expected to find a whoopee device. Indeed, he found a Bible, the NIV; "New Inflated Version" read the rubberized label implanted with a whistle. A diabolic sense of humor was at work, he smiled to himself as he looked about the room, but he would not give anyone the satisfaction of responding aloud. He would have put it on a lamp table if there weren't a Bible there already. In fact, there were Bibles of all sizes and shapes, all paraphrases and translations, lying on every flat space. He put it back under the cushion and slowly walked to the other side of the lobby.

"I like the snow," said Magdalene Smith, shivering; she had flown from New Orleans that afternoon with only a sweater to keep her warm, her husband having discouraged her from taking a coat or a jacket to the mountains when it was still ninety degrees in the Crescent City. She was *in* the world but not *of* it, an advertising executive who persisted in writing books on contemplative prayer. At moments of distraction, she imagined what it would be like if she were Teresa of Avila and her husband were John of the Cross.

"We must be the *token* Catholics," said S. J. Smith to everyone he met, thinking he knew how to make Evangelicals laugh. He was a contributing editor of a trade journal in the publishing industry that devoted unsold advertising space to religious books. He also did anthologies entitled *The Blankety-Blank Christian,* varying the adjective from volume to volume, and he claimed—to everyone's annoyance—that he knew everything there was to know about C. S. Lewis. "Just call me Smitty," he said to d'Esprit; she did not offer her hand.

"Fake," sniffed Hastings at the dried flowers, brushes, and mallows poking artistically out of a twenty-five-gallon milk can.

"If you so much as put your hand into your pocket," Magdalene whispered to Smitty, "I'll never speak to you again!"

"I was just reaching for my handkerchief," Smitty replied aloud, making no attempt to whisper, the fingers of his left hand slipping from silk zucchetto to Irish linen. In the past, to enliven dull ecumenical gatherings, he had been known to produce from his pocket a scarlet skullcap and do imitations of Roman Catholic cardinals.

"Are these for real?" asked Hastings, having bumped into the hostess of Christhaven, whose virgin wool sweater clung rather too willingly to her athletic form.

"Oh, they're for real, all right," she said cheerily. "This one is *Maranta kerchveana,* and this one is *Maranta massangeana.* They're prayer plants. Say hello to—I don't think we've been properly introduced. My name is Felicity French."

"Harold Hastings."

"Say hello to Mr. Hastings, girls," she said, watering them generously. "The reason I put them by the picture windows here is so that they can take advantage of the dark."

"You must mean the light," corrected Hastings, never missing an opportunity to exercise his superior intellect.

"No, I mean, the dark. During the day the leaves flop and fall about every which way. But during the night, they stand up straight and stretch toward the sky. Look, you can see their little burgundy undersides now."

"No," said Hastings, withdrawing from the conversation, "I don't think I want to do that."

From another corner of the lobby came the wobbling notes of "A Mighty Fortress," accompanied by snare drum and saxophone. Dolph Adolphssohn was at the keyboard of Arpeggio Magic, a small organ whose miniaturized circuits could reproduce the sounds of a polka band or a symphony orchestra. He was fingering the keyboard from memory, the sheet music on the rack in front of him "Country Pops" and "Top Pops," "easy play special music anyone can read 'n' play on sight."

"Don't you hate it when they thank you for not smoking," said Hastings to Adolphssohn, snapping in two a plastic strip provided by the American Cancer Society. "I'd give a good deal to replace all these stupid signs with 'Thank you for smoking—The American Tobacco Company'!"

"I don't smoke," said Adolphssohn without missing a beat. He was a Lutheran pastor, extravagantly educated in trivia and quadrivia, who wrote barnyard allegories and children's stories that inspired awe and quieted fear. "And neither should you. It's bad for your health."

"I feel my asthma coming on," said Smitty, who had worked for twenty years in New York City. "The air up here is just too clean." He had grasped Hastings by the arm and was trying to share his contempt for the cleaner life. "I've got to have industrial pollution in my nostrils, or I'll choke." Hastings managed to escape his grasp. "And I don't mind telling you, any of you, that I must have petroleum products in my drinking water or—"

"Let me give you a hug," said Wesley Willer, a Baptist minister from western Wyoming who looked and even sounded like Vincent Price about to host a horror show. He wrote popular spirituality and science fiction and once surprised his wife with a bound book on the wonderfulness of their marriage to celebrate their twenty-fifth wedding anniversary.

"That tickles," said Shirley Kerns as the Willer beard whiskered her cheek. She was cute and cuddly, and if she weren't such an observant Evangelical, she would have been the target of all these lonely males away from home. She too wrote children's stories for fiction, and for faction she described in moving terms the refugee camps she had visited around the world.

"Oh look," said Magdalene, picking up a magazine—one of many, all of them the latest—from the rack hanging on the side of the fireplace.

"Don't say it," warned Hastings.

"Don't say what?"

"'On a clear day you can see *Eternity!*'"

"I wasn't going to say that."

"That's a relief."

"I was going to say, '*Virtue* can't hurt you.'"

"That's even worse."

Arthur Stevens was slow to mix with the others. Leaning against the fireplace, he glanced occasionally at the bookcases, graveyards for *Reader's Digest* condensed books, biographies of Christian athletes, and nineteenth-century Bible commentaries. None of his published fantasy books appeared on the shelves, and he had the feeling that none of his soon-to-be published trilogy on the Arthurian legend would appear there either.

"I bet the pieces are missing," said Hastings to no one in particular, rummaging through the game boxes—Kismet, The Boss Game, Ten Commandments Bible Game—on top of the bookcases.

"I hope they have Zamphir," said d'Esprit, flipping through the audio cassettes stashed in a lowboy. "Nothing else gets the meditative juices flowing so lustily, I find."

"I would have thought you'd prefer Gregorian," said Magdalene.

"Oh, I like the chant, don't misunderstand me, but the piping notes of the Pan flute, well, they're just so . . . so pagan!"

"*I* prefer Johnny Mathis."

As the grandfather clock stroked the hour, a woodsman appearing at the top and swinging his ax six times into a chime shaped like a stump, the last vanload of guests arrived from the airport fifty miles down the mountain. From Illinois, swaddled in fur like a snow princess, came the poet Agatha Gaines; with her husband, who had died within the year, she founded a publishing house, which in a dozen years had issued, among other things, several slender volumes of her own silvery poetry. With her in the van should have been Whitewater Rivers, the Texas publisher who had funded the writer's conference even though his company did not publish any of the invited writers; he had missed connections in Denver and might now have to complete his trip by canoe or kayak, perhaps even by snowmobile.

"Are you ready?" asked Felicity, the hostess of Christhaven, who was standing by the door to the dining room. Her slender fingers were busily engaged, sculpting starched dinner napkins into alphas and omegas, lammikins and butterflies, and other intricacies of Christian symbology. "Is everyone here?"

"I think so," said Gloster. "Tell us what we do next. Eat, I hope. Everyone is starving."

"On behalf of the staff at Christhaven, I want to thank you all for coming," she said, tugging at her sweater. It had a tendency to rise; the panting hart of the Psalms, which decorated the sweater front, strained upward for liquid nourishment. "Before we go in to dinner, let me explain a few things to you. Your dinner is buffet. Tonight we are having Poulet à la Pikes Peak, with mountain vegetables and wild rice from my native state of Louisiana. By the way, I'd like to thank whoever it was who left the box of pralines under my pillow; that was very sweet. . . ."

"That wasn't me," whispered Smitty to his wife.

"I'll have your hands off at the wrists!"

"Your dishes are piled on this trestle table under the red cloth," said Felicity, her fingers pinching a corner of it. "After grace, please pick up a plate and proceed to the buffet. Then enter the dining room and choose a table. You'll find places already set with cutlery and glasses. Tea and coffee, with caffeine and without, you'll find along the wall. There's ice in the buckets."

"And icicles on the eaves," moaned Hastings. "It's freezing in here."

"Your fire I'll light after dinner," said Felicity, not wanting to waste an hour's worth of flame with no one in front of it. "Now, if we'll all join hands, I'll say a word of grace. Heavenly Father, we thank you for bringing us together. . . ."

As she led the group in prayer, Gloster glanced around and counted ten others. He was the eleventh. But where was the twelfth, Nathaniel Yates, the writer whose several books had only recently made pain a popular topic of polite conversation? Something of a pain himself to those who knew him, he was probably napping in bed, ignoring the rest of them, only to make a noisy entrance at midnight.

"As we partake this evening of our simple fare, we remember those less fortunate around the world who have nothing to put into their mouths. . . ."

As the grace lengthened, some wondered why they had been invited and looked forward to the revelation they felt sure would take place after dinner by the fire. Others gazed hungrily at the poster over the trestle, a banquet table extending toward infinity, with the words *Come, for all is now ready* superimposed over the picture.

"This we ask through Jesus' name. Amen."

She snapped the red cloth covering the dishes, the cloth-hitting-cloth sounding like a rifle crack.

Felicity screamed.

Instead of stacks of stoneware on the polished maple trestle, there lay a body, its limbs composed as if by a mortician or a movie director.

"Yipes!" shouted Hastings.

"No!" yelled Gloster. "Yates!"

He looked dead. He felt cold. There was a sprig of parsley in his lapel. Slipped between his limp fingers was a metallic sign with PERHAPS TODAY printed on it. The first word had been deleted in red, not by a messy smear but by a stroke so smart that, looking at it, one could almost hear the squeak of lipstick on alloy.

Chapter 2

WITHOUT ONE PLEA

ROBERT SIEGEL

"It was a dark and stormy night," Philippa d'Esprit mouthed silently over the book she'd plucked from the shelf. Chrysoprase and jasper flashed from her fingers where they curled around the glossy paperback. At the end of this, its first sentence, she sniffed audibly and raised one eyebrow. How many times *had* this sentence begun a book? she wondered, remembering the caveat uttered by her professor at Vassar. In defiance, she had used it once herself and sold half a million copies. She turned to the title page: "*Bible Stories for Hyperactive Children,* by Samson Jonah Smith"; and to the verso, "Copyright © 1986."

"Plagiarist!" she sniffed again. Then a slow, pickerel smile stretched along her cheek as she realized Smitty must have planted the book there upon his arrival. She turned back to the first page and continued. "The wind shrieked through the rigging while the boat's ribs cracked and popped like the knees of Pharisees rising from prayer. . . ."

Philippa sniffed a third time, wrinkling her brow as she slammed the book shut. What some people wouldn't do for lucre—the miserable thief! Even the Gospels weren't safe, for God's sake! Once they drew and quartered people for such sacrilege! Closing her eyes, she yearned intensely for the thirteenth century. For a moment all grew dark, and she saw in the distance a flat gold sky under which a unicorn impaled an avaricious scribe . . . but the scene blurred. She opened her eyes; it was still 1986. She sighed, for the moment chained to the present. Smitty's book had brought back the unpleasantness of the last hour too vividly. A void opened in her stomach as she thought of Yates's gray corpse. "'Oh keep the Dog far hence, that's friend to men'"—she quoted T. S. Eliot, the Anglican, who himself was quoting an earlier Anglican—"'Or with his nails he'll dig it up again!'" She shivered. "'The supplication of a dead man's hand. . . .'"

Turning to face the others, for a moment she was blinded by the fire crackling in the open hearth. She averted her eyes to where its light brushed across the ceiling like huge archangelic wings stabbed at by shadows from corners. Weakening, she grasped a chair arm. *Like fallen angels,* she said to herself, looking around at the others, slumped in chairs or standing in the flickering light. *Pandemonium . . . No—more like children whose party's been spoiled.*

George Gloster meditated, returning his gaze to the center of the flames. All flesh was grass, he reflected, grass for the burning—for a moment reminded of summer in Kansas. It was the postcard of this limestone fireplace under a ceiling with exposed beams that had drawn him to consider Christhaven in the first place. It seemed ideal for a conference, close to a major ski resort town, not far from Pikes Peak. On a knoll, it commanded spectacular views in every direction.

The lodge itself was what a real estate agent friend of Gloster's would call "chaletsy." Felicity French had insisted on showing all of it to all of the guests when they arrived, despite their polite—and, in one case, not-so-polite—protests. There was a central lobby-cum-living room rising two stories and surrounded by a balcony off which most of the bedrooms opened. Taken together, these rooms could sleep thirty comfortably or, if the roommates were not of the same family, uncomfortably. Outside the bedrooms, exposed to the wilderness scene, with Pikes Peak visible from one angle, was a deck that ran around all four sides of the building. Inside, a flight of stairs led to an unfinished third story and a large flat roof used in summers for barbecues. Some of the roof was rotting, confessed Felicity, after Smitty had stepped through a deck-board. If it weren't for the murder, thought Gloster, as he stared through the flames of the two-way fireplace at the far side of the living room, the lodge was the perfect choice for the conference. Comfortable but not ostentatious. Of course, John Woolman would not have approved of the heated swimming pool. Yes, smiled Gloster mischievously, the world was corrupt, and they all were touched by that corruption. But things were bound to change, and Christhaven was, but for the shock of Yates's abrupt departure for the next world, the perfect place for that change to begin.

A little shriek interrupted his meditation. He ducked as something soft bounced off his shoulder into the fire. Shirley Kerns rushed forward to save a small pillow from the flames, and a nasty laugh erupted from Hastings, boyish and blond reclining on the sofa.

"Don't bother, Shirl," he drawled. "It's a synthetic fabric."

Ignoring him, Shirley picked up the tongs and reached for the pillow.

Pow-pow-pow-pow-pow, a string of small explosions rattled, apparently from the pillow. Shirley dropped the tongs and fled from the room.

"Holy Cow!" shouted Hastings, sitting up.

"Why did you do that?" demanded Gloster.

"How was I to know it was loaded?" Hastings shrugged and lay back down. Gloster glanced at the shriveled black remains. How quickly it had melted in the fire, and how awful it smelled!

Barely an hour had passed since the body had been discovered. Bowls of cooling clam chowder, hardly touched, sat near each of the conferees. Felicity hovered over one or another, encouraging each to take nourishment for body and soul.

"Oh, my dears," she said in sorrowful tones, "the flock must feed, even when one of its members. . . ." Her voice trailed off, unable to locate an exact Gospel parallel.

". . . has been seized by the wolf," Gloster said under his breath. He was amazed at how this young hostess had handled the moment at the trestle table. After removing the cloth, she'd let out a scream worthy of a Zouave at Shiloh but had not fainted or even paused. She'd replaced the cloth over the body, even tucking in the edges, and ordered everybody out of the dining room, told the cook to stay in the kitchen, and then telephoned the sheriff's office.

Gathering them together in the living room, she had said, "All of us at Christhaven are terribly shocked and sorrowful at what has happened. We want to assure you that this sort of thing has never happened before here, and we trust it shall never happen again. We know also that the Lord is here and what is dark shall be made light and the sorrowing shall be comforted." She paused. "Meanwhile, Cook and I will serve dinner to you again out here."

Cook appeared bearing a tray of steaming bowls.

Felicity bowed her head. "Lord, we hold up to you the soul of Mr. Yates and pray that you will receive him into your bosom." She sighed and shook her dark curls. "We pray for his bereaved family and also for the benighted soul of the person or persons who took his life. Amen. Now, let's all say the Twenty-third Psalm. . ."

Masterful, Gloster thought—he couldn't have done better himself. At the words "shall dwell in the house of the Lord forever," Agatha Gaines burst into loud sobs and left, supported to her room by Willer and Smitty. But the others sat about, stuporous, waiting for the sheriff to arrive.

Meniscus became membrane in the milky bowls that were mostly untouched. Magdalene Smith bent over her rosary, apparently reciting the sorrowful mysteries. As Gloster ambled by, he thought he saw a drop of blood ooze between the knuckles of her right hand, clenched tightly about a crucifix.

At a corner desk, jaw muscles twitching, Adolphssohn hunched over a piece of paper, drawing a serpent, a mythological *wyrm*, its coils circling the borders of the paper, its fanged head jutting into the middle. The dark coils squeezed a shrinking white space at the center.

The woodsman in the grandfather clock solemnly swung his ax eight times, and still no sheriff arrived. Several members of the conference slipped from the lobby and descended to the floor below, whence soon came sounds of balls in play, both billiard and Ping-Pong. And from the kitchen came the plangent tones of Felicity's voice, rising and falling as if she were coaxing someone to fill his mouth with food.

Gloster glanced down at his gelid soup, then quickly away. He thought of Yates's grayish corpse stretched out on a table in the dining room like an unholy offering to cannibals. But weren't all writers cannibals? A bloodthirsty bunch, savaging each other behind the back, especially in reviews. And publishers, didn't they often drink the lifeblood of writers through ridiculous royalties and remaindering clauses? Religious publishers were the worst of all, exploiting writers under the rubric of evangelical poverty. Next to this sort of exploitation, murder could almost be considered justifiable homicide.

Yes, Woolman and Christ were right about that, the love of money was the root of evil. But what did money provide, except power? Here a squeal from the kitchen nearly derailed his meditation. No, one couldn't discount sex, of course; it was the third of the big three: money, power, and sex. But compared to the others, sex was a bauble, a ruinous plaything, as the history of the world showed. Power—used rightly—was the one, and he had been given the power in this meeting to begin to change things. Staring into the fire he rested his chin on his fist.

Soon he heard the kitchen's swing door squeak open, and in another moment Livingston Johns hove into view, wiping his mouth on his sleeve.

Johns found Felicity's blandishments hard to resist and followed her into the kitchen where she warmed up her Poulet à la Pikes Peak.

"After all," she'd admonished, handing him a hot plate, "the Lord wants us to keep up our strength in times of crisis."

"My sentiments exactly," replied Johns, sinking his teeth into a flaky slice of breast. "As Gandalf says, if more of us valued *mmf* good food, good *mmf* friends, and good *mmf* cheer, the world would be a better *ermf* place. Do you like hobbits?"

"I adorrre the fuzzy little critters!" Felicity said, flashing a smile warmer than Old Hickory's powder pan at the Battle of New Orleans.

"Well," he said, tucking in a bit of thigh, "I think Tolkien is the Spenser of our day."

"I don't know about Spenser. But I know y'all write books, too," she said, hugging herself. "I think that must be wonderful!" The reference to his books sent Johns into a monologue too long to recount here. He ended by quoting Keats's "Ode on a Grecian Urn" and two of his own poems in their entirety. While he recited, his chicken cooled and had to be reheated by Felicity.

How delightful it was, reflected Johns as he entered the lobby, when literary intelligence was found in out-of-the-way places! With only an associate degree in hotel management from Fort Bliss Community College, Felicity had the makings of a first-class graduate student in English. Among the hundreds of students he had taught at a large midwestern university, few exhibited her immediate, sensuous grasp of poetry. "'Full many a rose is born to blush unseen,'" he quoted, suppressing a burp, "'And waste its fragrance on the desert air.'" He tripped on a leg of the coffee table, caught himself, and eased into a pillowed rocker near Willer.

Willer lay at one end of the sofa, his face buried in a pillow. Suddenly he sat up and stared into the fire. "At a time like this," he intoned, clutching the pillow to his middle, "the only comfort is the closeness of another human being." He swung about toward Shirley Kerns, seated at the other end of the sofa, one fuzzy, white, cowgirl-boot slipper crossed over the other. The corner of his eye glinted in the flames. "I need to *hug* someone, Shirl," he pleaded, extending both arms.

As if she hadn't heard, Shirley drew her legs under her, crossed her arms over her light blue cashmere, and closed her eyes. Her white dickey couldn't have looked more ecclesiastical on John Donne himself, Johns decided. Willer's arms dropped leadenly to his sides, and he swung about to stare at the fire again, pupils shrinking to pinpoints in the glare.

Johns's sympathies lay with Kerns as he recalled the story his editor at Cross-Purposes once told him over a lunch of Lasagna Rigoletto. The publisher's motto ("For the Purpose of the Cross") and logo (a crusader's cross circled by a crown of thorns) appeared on Kerns's books and, indeed, on the books of several others invited to the conference. Between red leaves of Salatto Rappuchini, his editor recounted how an overzealous sales manager changed the title of one of Kerns's books from *Open Hearth, Open Home*—the subject was Christian hospitality—to *Open Hug, Open Heart.* The result was that Kerns, speaking to a conference of switched-on Charismatics, wound up in a hospital with three cracked ribs. The book sold 50,000 copies in three weeks; her ½% royalty was enough to pay the doctor's bill, but not the hospital's. Since then she'd grown progressively wary of the Christian hug.

Johns stared out the back windows where snowflakes like pinched, white faces appeared briefly before dissolving in the dark. They fell straight down in a momentary lull of the winds sweeping from the Continental Divide. He stared, but after a while he no longer saw, failing to observe the sliding glass door opening and an enormous woman with Balkan features, swaddled in an enormous fur coat, entering the room from the sun deck. So deft were her movements that no one else turned to see who it was. She made her way behind them all and disappeared through the door to the swimming pool.

"When is that sheriff going to get here?" shouted Hastings, who in his nervousness was stripping leaves off the second *Maranta.* The first prayer plant was a denuded twig.

"Shortly, or not at all, in this blizzard," said Gloster, tossing another log on the fire and jumping back from the sparks.

Someone cleared her throat on the balcony, and they all looked up. "Is it too early for an elegy?" asked Agatha Gaines as she descended the stairs. "I've written a poem about Nate that I want to share with you." *Too early,* nodded everyone in the lobby. "Later, of course," she said, stuffing the piece of paper into her pocket and returning to her room on the second floor.

"Oh my!" said Willer, stretching and standing up. "Is anyone else in a mood to share who we are and why we're here?" He looked hopefully at Shirley.

"I wish none of us were here," Shirley said, pulling a long face. "At least I wish *I* wasn't."

"You and me both, kiddo," Hastings agreed, as he stripped the last leaf from the second *Maranta.*

"No, Wesley, I don't think this is the right time to share," said Magdalene Smith, her face floating in the shadows with the radiant pallor of an El Greco. "I need silence," she said, a rosary wreathing her fingers. "I'm going upstairs."

"An excellent idea," said Philippa, who had been dozing for the last half hour. Shirley joined the procession. Most of the men agreed that they needed diversion, not silence, and headed downstairs to table hockey.

That left Johns and Lynne Teal, Gloster's assistant, sitting in the lobby. It was she who had planned the meeting and looked after the practical needs of the group. So self-effacing was she that she was scarcely noticed by the others. Her pencil raced across a stenographer's notebook, rearranging the schedule for the following day, trying to salvage the conference if she could.

Hopelessly unathletic, Johns opted to sit by the fireplace. For the first time he noticed that there was more than one clock sounding the hour. A woodsman chopped the hour in the lobby clock, but on the second floor he heard another, sweeter sound, chimes playing the first nine notes of a familiar hymn. Try as he might he couldn't recall the words, but he'd heard them many times in college chapel.

He was glad to be alone, to have time to consider the whole situation. Who did it? he wondered. No one had asked aloud the question that was on everyone's mind. With apologies to Yates, it was an almost perfect mystery. Each of the guests had a plausible motive. Each of them might have killed Yates. It was another instance of life imitating literature, and perhaps literary analysis could help him. Teaching in an English department that seized upon every new twitch and flutter of French critical fashion, Johns secretly preferred literature itself to the critics who fattened on it like so many ticks. Nevertheless, he was intrigued by criticism's recent veering toward philosophy, its radical critique of language and the ordinary view of *reality.* One esoteric strand showed how everything, in the last analysis, *was* language. This notion flattered his own intuitions and agreed with the extreme value put on the word in Christian tradition. "In the beginning was the Word," was the way the corduroy professor began many a class. Poetry, fantasy, so-called realistic fiction—what were they but truer, that is, *more meaningful,* constructions than ordinary life, itself a fictional construct of the mind? And what made the mind but language? Language made language: the word made the world. *I am the Alpha and the Omega. . . .* "And any one of us might have created the crime," Johns murmured to the fire as the fat woman in the enormous furs emerged from the swimming pool door and tiptoed behind him to the sliding door and snow-drifted deck beyond. "It all depends on the words one chooses."

Gloster, for instance, could well have envied Yates, who was another contender, so to speak, in the ring of spiritual non-fiction. . . .

Philippa, head of a national writers' guild and easily the most famous of the present company, might be out to put the kibosh on this group the way Herod took precautionary measures at Bethlehem. . . .

Hastings had reason to hate other writers. He'd suffered contractual abuse by a famous convert whose ghostwritten books had earned the convert millions but barely kept Hastings in liquid paper. . . .

S. J. Smith—known to his intimates, Johns had learned, as "Society of Jesus" Smith—had once been a member of a religious order known for infiltrating Protestant organizations and doing things worth burning at the stake for. . . .

His wife, however, was an unknown quantity; Magdalene could obviously pray, oblivious to her own blood—and perhaps that of others. . . .

Adolphssohn had already confessed that he and Yates had agreed to meet for three days in Denver following the conference to trade ideas. . . .

Agatha Gaines, who had just become sole owner of a publishing house, might possibly think that the conference spelled the end of the exploitation of writers by religious publishers; to maintain the highest profitability on the bottommost line, she might even kill.

He couldn't dismiss Arthur Stevens; like Magdalene, he was hard to figure out; deep in studies of alchemic lore, he had flown all the way from Wales to attend this meeting. Wasn't such an effort a trifle gregarious for the recluse he claimed to be? Johns remembered alchemy's ancient slogan, "Not a few have perished in our work."

Nor could he overlook Shirley Kerns, who wrote chiefly nonfiction and competed in the same markets as Yates for the all-too-few lucrative assignments.

Willer was just too nice; the book he had written to his wife celebrating their marriage was enough to make him a prime suspect in Johns's mind. Such an excess of uxoriousness would have hanged a man in the time of King Henry VIII.

He had to consider Lynne Teal, Gloster's assistant, pin-neat, composed, and amused as she quietly watched their behavior, attentive as a mother duck to her noisy brood. For what purpose was she always taking notes? Could she and Gloster be a murderous twosome?

He could not—alas—dismiss the thought of Felicity French. She had seemed almost too composed, too much in control, after the initial surprise. Did her literary acumen, abundant charm, and obvious passion sheathe the steely compulsion of a killer? A tremor moved up Johns's long frame as he thought of dying in her arms. A consummation devoutly to be wished?

He sighed. Whom had he forgotten? There were, of course, the cook and the kitchen help and, of course, himself. He too had a motive. His dissertation on the problem of evil had lain unpublished all these years, but now Yates was attempting to corner the market on evil with a popular book on the subject. Passages, it seemed to Johns, had been lifted right out of his dissertation and thinly disguised.

He picked up from the coffee table a copy of Yates's book, *When Bad Things Happen to Bad People.* What macabre wit had placed it there? A sardonic memorial indeed! Yates's thesis was that, since we are all sinners in the eyes of God, all of us are bad. Therefore, none of us should be surprised when bad things happen to us. On the contrary, we should take grim comfort in the fact that justice has been done; it shows that Providence is alert and working, taking care of its own. Yates had supposedly scrounged through forgotten theologians from the Swiss Reformation to colonial New England for refinements of this argument—though Johns suspected he'd cribbed it all from recent histories of theology.

To illustrate his thesis, Yates filled the book with examples of murderers and other malefactors going ecstatically to the block or gallows; of wastrels who died rapturously in sackcloth, delighted to be consumed by their own excesses; pirates, who atoned for feeding virgins to the sharks by embracing the hangman; stranglers who kissed the axman's hands; and even a young nobleman, guilty of incestuous rape, who'd asked St. Catherine of Siena to catch his head in her lap when it leaped from the block. Not for three centuries, Johns suspected, had hyper-Calvinism been so refurbished and burnished as in Yates's book. After reading it, Calvin himself might have shuddered and flung himself at the feet of the pope. Yet the book was admirably, if morbidly, consistent. In fact, its reasoned morbidity made Yates a prime suspect in his own murder.

Pleased with his survey of the suspects, Johns reached into his jacket pocket and extracted a slim volume. It was his own book of poems, memorializing a wet and—alas—extended vacation he'd taken on the west coast of Ireland. He had titled it *Innipiggserse,* after the Gaelic fishing village where he'd spent eight damp and lonely weeks courting his muse. In seven shades of green and modeled after the script of the illuminated Book of Kells, the title glowed on an ivory background. Johns ran his fingers over it lovingly, then opened the cover. If Gaines were going to read a poem for Yates, then he would too. He slowly turned the pages. Here was an appropriate one, "To Market, To Market," with its epigraph from Mother Goose:

> To market, to market
> To buy a fat pig.

He smiled, settled deeper into the cushion, and soon was totally absorbed.

A few minutes later he looked up and listened, as if he heard something at a distance. He shut the book and strode from the room.

The fire creaked and waned, the coals taking individual outline, each darkening perimeter closing on a radiant center until the center lay eclipsed—except for occasional fits of light inspired by drafts from the windows.

The fire was down to its last red eye when Johns settled once again on the sofa. He sat motionless and stared a long time at the winking coal. His reverie was interrupted by a shrill cry from the kitchen.

"Water! There's *water* coming through the ceiling! It's Room 17, I think!" Felicity's voice was joined immediately by a confusion of tongues. The kitchen door burst open. She and several others pounded up the stairs in a flurry. Johns caromed up the staircase after them as fast as his ample frame would allow.

"Is someone in there?" Felicity called out, knocking loudly. As Johns cleared the landing, other doors were opening and heads popping out along the corridor. Felicity rattled the door to Room 17. "Please open up!"

"Stand back!" Johns called out, running down the corridor. Several scrambled out of his way.

THUD—he bounced off the door and luckily caught himself on the railing. He stifled a moan and rubbed his arm as Felicity took keys from her pocket and unlocked the door.

Johns could hear water running over the tub as the group crowded through the door toward the bathroom. The inner door was open and the light on. In front of him Felicity cried, "Oh, no!" and slumped to the floor.

Johns peered over Adolphssohn. There, water running over the edge of the tub, a white plastic bib around its neck, floated the wide-eyed, naked corpse of a stranger.

"Who—" he started, interrupted by an incredulous voice behind him.

"That's—that's—Whitewater Rivers!"

"But it can't be!" shrieked Lynne Teal. "He hasn't arrived yet. He's supposed to be snowed in at the airport."

"Quick, let's get him out!" Adolphssohn said. As Johns and Adolphssohn dragged the publisher to the bedroom floor, they saw words scrawled, as if in red crayon, on the bib: JUST AS I AM.

Gloster and Adolphssohn began mouth-to-mouth resuscitation on Whitewater. Johns knelt by the inert form of Felicity French and did his best to revive her. Absorbed in his work and making some progress—her left eyelid had fluttered—he heard the clock in the corridor strike ten. Again, the chimes played the hymn.

"That's it!" he said in a whisper as he leaned forward, pressing the breath from her rib cage; and then, crouched down, his mouth approaching her dark, open one, he murmured, "Just as I am, without one plea."

Chapter 3

THE SHEPHERD WHO CAME IN FROM THE COLD

WALTER WANGERIN, JR.

It was not in S. J. Smith's character *not* to be where the action was. He was drawn to motion as a wandering, purposeless eye settles on things moving. And though he liked to consider himself an observer, not a joiner, he would float at the edges of any fray he found, making ironic comments on the event—to himself, if no one else was interested in listening.

But when things exploded in Room 17 at 10 P.M. that snowy night, when the body of Whitewater Rivers was found afloat in the bathtub, when men bolted from the basement to see why Felicity French had screamed and why Livingston Johns had woofed like a bear aroused midwinter, it happened that Smitty was sitting on the toilet, unable to make haste.

Haste this short man made in secret. Insouciance was the mask he wore in public. Near panic he felt in private when he thought that he was missing something. Wry indifference he presented to the people when at last he arrived at the scene of that something.

Therefore, when matters were concluded in the basement bathroom, Smitty burst from the door, lowered his head, and bulleted up the steps into the main lounge, breathing heavily through his nose. He whirled round to the next staircase, to the action still thumping and chattering, splashing and rumbling upstairs in the bedrooms, but motion caught his eye near the kitchen door, at the trestle table just outside the dining room door: the drop of the cloth that covered Yates's body, the withdrawal of a human arm into shadow.

Smitty froze at the staircase, his eye cast backward.

"Somebody there?"

Yates was a corpse, after all. Corpses do change the atmosphere of common places and cause even sophisticated people a certain disquiet at a question unanswered, a movement unaccounted for. Corpses do make shadows seem premonitory, and when cool Smitty repeated the question, he sounded positively nervous, belligerent.

"Is somebody there?"

The figure of a man emerged beside the trestle table, thin, slouching, and faceless in the dim light.

"Arthur Stevens?" Smitty asked. The man's form was closer to Stevens's than anyone else's—except Yates, who was both thin and dead.

The man was watching Smitty, observing, in no hurry to answer.

Smitty turned around fully, then, and hung a careless smile on his face. "Some of us," he said casually, "don't rush to every noise we hear, right? Some of us can live without the bother, right, Stevens? The cooler heads shall prevail. . . ."

The dark man took a step forward into light. Smitty squeaked and jumped backward. "I thought you were Stevens!"

"You thought wrong," he drawled in a baritone voice. "Who are you?"

"Smith."

"There's a name don't help me much."

"Smith," said Smitty, making the *S* sound precious through a nervous lisp. "Samson Jonah Smith."

"Not a whole lot better. And this," drawled the stranger, lifting the cloth from Yates's face, "is the victim, I take it. I suppose you figured to do right by him and laid him out on a table. Dignified. Proper. You're all writers, Sam?"

"Not Sam. S. J. Smith!" The stranger's barb had snapped him into his public image of mild disdain. "Yes, we are writers. No, we did not lay Yates on the table. We know better than to disturb the scene of a murder. Who, sir, are you? A cowboy?"

This stranger was loose, round-shouldered, and had a lunging blade of a narrow nose, sunken cheeks, sunken eyes, weathered skin, and ruinous white string for hair. His motion was slow: slowly he rolled the red cloth down the length of Yates's body.

"This the way you found him?"

"Yes."

"Ah. Dramatic stunt. To leave the victim balanced on his own viewing table. And someone left a sign here, I see: PERHAPS TODAY. Or just TODAY. Sort of like a title, hey? A caption, wouldn't you say? Like to a picture or a story?"

"Who are you?"

"Well, I ain't a cowboy," said the stranger, still gazing at Yates's corpse. "None of you touched the victim, you say?"

"That's exactly what I said."

"Yet lickety-split you all discerned two critical things, at a distance, as it were. But I s'pose writers can do that. One, the man's dead. Two, the man's been murdered. Three, call for the sheriff. All from eyeballing the man. Wonderful. Four," said the man, lifting his eyes to the balcony above, "have a party." Laughter was erupting from rooms on the second floor. "What are your people doing up there?"

"They're not my people," Smitty declared. "And I don't know what they're doing."

"Why don't we have a look-see, then?"

"Who are you, sir," Smitty repeated for the third time, backing out of the stranger's way, convinced he smelled animal sweat, "the sheriff?"

"Good Lord, no! I wouldn't run for no office." He began to mount the stairs. "Used to pan a little gold near Cripple Creek. Used to own a little livestock in the valleys." He paused and glanced down at Smitty. "Guess a writer would call me a shepherd."

"A shepherd?" Smitty had shouted so loud that the laughter quieted above and people stuck their heads over the balustrade to see what was going on. "A shepherd! What are you doing here?"

"Well," said the man, scratching his brown jaw, "I'm the only one could get through the snow. Me and my mule. The sheriff's my son-in-law, slow and modern in most things. But he had the wit to call me when you all called him. My name's George Bent."

"Smitty," called Gloster from above, "is that the sheriff?"

"The man's a shepherd."

"Naw," Bent said slowly as he climbed the stairs to the crowd on the balcony. "Not anymore. Been mostly trapping, lately. Me and my mule. So, this is what writers look like."

Writers. Some stood on the balcony. Some stood and some sat in Room 17. One or two peeped out of the bathroom.

Johns was holding a handkerchief to his nose, soaking a flow of blood with it. Felicity was wringing her hands and looking upon Johns with woeful apology. She had awakened from her swoon to find the bear above her, preparing to puff another breath into her mouth—and she punched him in the face. That was the cause of the previous laughter.

But the laughter had come so easily because of the nervous tension all suffered at the moment. Gloster was on the balcony, fairly panting with the sense of responsibility: he had gathered the group in the first place, but matters had been snatched from his hands, snatched savagely and twice, and he felt helpless to know how to explain himself or to restore order in a conference veering crazily toward death. He could have handled disputes regarding literature or Christianity or self-centered pride. He could have calmed a load of theoretical sin. But the sin itself unmanned him, made him pant.

Adolphssohn and Hastings both were dripping water on the floor of Room 17. Their shirtsleeves clung to their arms, their pantlegs were hiked above their ankles and wet. In front of them was Willer, kneeling, as though he had brought an offering into a holy place. Beside him was Whitewater Rivers, his mouth pinched open into a soundless cry—a sort of a yawn—by Willer's fingers.

On the bed sat Shirley, fanning herself, tears on her cheeks from crying or laughing or fear or sympathy—who could tell? Next to her, Agatha, a piece of paper in her hand, some neat printing and a poem on the paper.

Philippa stood monumental beside the bathroom door, a circle of absolute calm in the midst of this picture of frozen, bewildering activity.

And, peeping from the bathroom door were three mysterious spirits: Stevens, Magdalene, and Lynne.

"So," said Bent, gazing from person to person in the diorama, "this is what writers look like. I can't say as I yearned much to know. But I will admit, you make a sight I'd hate to miss."

Smitty said, "Who's that? Who have you been hugging now, Willer?"

Gloster said, "In Heaven's name, why did they send a shepherd when we called for the sheriff?"

Willer said, "This is Whitewater Rivers."

Shirley said, "Hugs can kill, but hugging didn't do this."

Felicity said, "He's not a shepherd. Are you a shepherd, Mr. Bent? I never knew you were a shepherd."

Smitty said, "Do what? What's the matter with Rivers? When did he come? Hugging didn't do what?"

Philippa said, "Peace to all publishers. Immortal peace."

Gloster said, "If he isn't a shepherd, what is he? When will we get an authority up here?"

Shirley said, "Nothing personal, people, but I'm leaving tomorrow."

Willer said, "He's dead."

Adolphssohn said, "Drowned."

Hastings shot Adolphssohn an immediate look. "We don't know that."

Johns said, "I think he said he was a trapper. Didn't you say you were a trapper, not a shepherd?"

Magdalene said, "Do you mind? I came into the facility to use it, not to gawk. Stevens, do you mind?"

Gloster shouted, "Trapper, shepherd, whatever! For Pete's sake, where's the sheriff?"

"Dead?" said Smitty. "Rivers is dead? That's two of you."

"Two of *us*, Smith," said Hastings.

Agatha said, "How soon is too soon for an elegy?"

Philippa said, "I'll go with you, Shirley. There's no point to staying any—"

All at once the sliding glass door to the outside deck rolled open. A terrific wind blasted into the room, snatching the paper from Agatha's hand and whirling the room full of snow. This same wind was howling outside, making the pine trees moan and whipping their boughs like arms both stiff and supplicating. The weather was a white violence. Even the wagon wheel chandelier in the lobby began to swing, animating the lobby below with shadow and twitching a thousand sprites.

Philippa had to grab her skirt, which was billowing like a spinnaker.

"Who?" cried Hastings, spinning around.

Bent rolled the glass door closed again and rubbed his jaw. He had opened it. He had ambled through the contumely of words and writers altogether unnoticed, had unlocked and opened the door to the elements; and now he stood bemused before writers blown silent.

"There's your answer, ladies," he said. "I don't expect anybody's going anywhere tomorrow. This here's a blizzard, and it isn't fixing to quit. As for you," he said to Gloster, "this blizzard's why you got me instead of my son-in-law. He'd fit in here, I'm sure. He's a university graduate. He'd know how to talk to the lot of you. But he doesn't have a mule, and I do—and I ain't without authority myself, seeing as how I've been deputized. And I've got three things on my side besides. Age: when you've been seeing folk as long as I have, you lose the fear of their opinion and start to see straight through them. Experience: since folk don't act much different from wolves and weasels, martens, fox, and the nervous hare, I've cracked a case or two in my time. 'Cracked a case.' That's how you writers say it, ain't it? My son-in-law chokes on the need, but he's called me in before. Now, about your corpses. . . ."

"You said 'three,' Mr. Bent."

"What?"

"'Three things.' You said you had 'three things' on your side. Excuse my doubt," said Gloster, "but I need as much persuasion as possible that you are able to handle this matter. A deputy isn't a sheriff, after all."

"No," said Bent slowly, "no, it ain't."

"And if age makes credibility, Philippa here is a peg or two your superior. Forgive me, Philippa. I'm acting under a strain," said Gloster.

"Yep," said Bent. "She beats me by a wrinkle."

"Neither does it inspire confidence that you know animals well enough to kill them. Three. I think I need to hear your third qualification."

"Fair enough," said Bent. He pulled out a mashed pouch of chewing tobacco and tucked a plug behind his lip. "Here's my third plus: I figure if I can talk to my mule and make her go through a blinding snowstorm uphill, I can talk to a writer as well."

Hastings was shivering helplessly, though he kept his eyes half-lidded. The wind had chilled his wet clothing.

"Boy, you need to dry yourself and get into bed," said Bent. "In fact, you all look a bit bedraggled to me. About your corpses. I've seen the one you telephoned about. Don't need no more looking there. You and you. What are your names?"

"Dolph Adolphssohn."

"Wesley Willer."

"Dolph, Wesley, and Sam Smith. Shoot!" Bent shook his head in wonder. "D'you all make up your own names? Dolph and Wesley, drag the downstairs body outside and sit him in a chair on the deck. Ain't no room in the freezer, and if you don't cool him down, he'll wake you with his smell. Give me ten minutes with this one up here, then come and get him, too."

"I'll help carrying," said Gloster, ever responsible.

"Yep, you'll help," said Bent, "but not with carrying. You're too jumpy and too short—and that one's bleeding at his snout, and that one's shivering in his breeches, and that one"—Arthur Stevens—"don't pay me no mind yet, though he will, and that one"—S. J. Smith—"is short and above it all at once. Dolph and Wesley, move the bodies. You, what's your name?"

"George Gloster."

"You, Gloster, hang around to give me information, the who and the why and the what of this here gathering of writers. Maybe my son-in-law's heard of one or the other of you. Women, women, go to bed. The rest of you, go to bed. Tonight, Miss Felicity, it's thirteen laying down their heads in your lodge. Pray God it's thirteen heads rise up tomorrow. Go."

Yates had a puff of curly hair all around his head, a triangular face, and a beard that brought his chin to a point. He looked like a wedge-shaped hoe, his body the handle. You'd think he'd be light. But his flesh and joints had begun the process of stiffening, and though he didn't flop in their hands, he oozed into odd shapes. Moreover, neither Adolphssohn nor Willer wanted to carry him as brusquely as one carries a mattress or a stag. He had been human, once, when he was writing. Their sensibilities, then, and the effort at human propriety made them mincing as they lifted him. He was a difficult load, and he slipped once or twice from their grasp. His head made a gruesome *thump* on the floor.

"He doesn't deserve this, you know," said Willer.

"You knew him?" Adolphssohn asked.

"I've read him. He was a precise writer and a good man. We're bouncing a Christian brain on the floor. Look out!"

Adolphssohn had Yates by the armpits and was backing up. The arms kept rising as if in a sleeping hosanna. When Adolphssohn tried to shift the load, he clattered backward into a chair, dropped Yates, and caught himself from falling. In a sudden fit of spectacular rage, Adolphssohn turned and kicked the chair at the front door. Four legs splintered into bits, and the seat itself split in two.

"Adolphssohn!" said Willer, astonished. "Control yourself."

"*Mea culpa*," the brooding Lutheran said. "I don't know how to hold this thing."

"No fun, this lugging the guts into the nether weather."

"No. No fun."

Willer always said that someone was "a good man," "a good woman." Willer never tired of petting people as though they were puppies, complimenting their Christianity, speaking edifying words regarding their characters, smiling as though all the world were a potluck supper and no one was terribly young or obnoxious, no one terribly old or doddering. Every citizen in Willer's kingdom made good casseroles.

Perhaps this had popped Adolphssohn's restraint. He saw the world iniquitous, all its righteousness as filthy rags. There lurked evil in the hearts both of the obnoxious children and the doddering ancients, evil in cooks and the keepers of hostelries and sidewinders whose sons-in-law were sheriffs, evil in the hearts of Christian writers, male and female. Dolph's own heart smoked with subterranean fires and his eye turned with suspicion on his confreres. He had grown, in the last hours, very tense.

"I understand, I understand," said Willer. "Everybody's edgy, half of us meeting for the first time, the weather unkind, imprisoning us, and two of our number have passed away. I understand why you might let off a little steam, Dolph. You're a good man at heart."

The requiescent Yates seemed to share a sardonic smile with the rug. All things held a mildly wicked humor for Yates, even death, even rugs, even Willer's busy, busy *good* humor.

Dolph saw the smirk and felt better.

"Let's try it again, Willer," he said. "Grab the ankles."

"Say, weren't you two going to hang around after the conference, you and Yates?"

"It was the plan."

"You knew him, then?"

"We were friends."

"Of course you'd feel the grief, then. What was Yates like?"

"I never had anything against him. He was a man of estimable organization. His hair was curly, but his life was combed, sharply parted. Writing was that part. He never wasted a word or a dime." They'd come to the front door. "Why do you ask? I thought you knew him, too."

"We met. We shared the podium at several conferences and seminars through the years. But, you know. What can you learn of someone in the public spotlight?"

"Did you know Rivers?"

"In passing. He never published any of my stuff. A good man, though. A good man."

The wind shrieked when Adolphssohn opened the door. It was as though the black beast had been waiting for opportunity. It stung the men's faces, took their breath away. They hunched their shoulders and entered the night.

Pine trees whistled and moaned above them. Drifts had thickened on the lee side of every standing thing, oblivious of sidewalks and paths. Willer and Adolphssohn had to lift their feet very high to trudge the snow, and the wind shot under their collars.

"Where will we leave him?" shouted Willer, his voice ripped the wrong way in the wind. No shed, no dignified retreat, no covering.

"How about that chair over there?"

"Out of the wind!" cried Adolphssohn.

They dragged Yates to the chair and forced his stiffening joints into a sitting position. Here the snow spiraled down crazily, softly, passing through shafts of yellow window light.

Adolphssohn, on a premonition, looked up and saw the figures of two women standing on the upper deck above him, bent over, gazing down.

"Who's that?" he asked Willer.

"Don't know," he said. "Hey, up there! You'll catch your death!"

Neither woman moved. They might have been effigies of watchfulness or of mourning. Their hair tugged leftward in the wind.

Upstairs, with less ceremony and less conversation, Adolphssohn and Willer simply wrapped Rivers in several blankets and dragged him down the stairs through the sliding doors out onto the deck and sat him in a chair.

Adolphssohn heard a persistent murmur behind the door of Room 21 as he went to his own room: Bent and Gloster in close discussion, the trapper catching information.

Behind the women's door he heard not a sound.

Shirley whispered in a low voice, a thrilling ring in her voice, "The snow is sifting into his eyes. Can you see that?"

Agatha whispered, "No, I can't see as well as you."

They stood in the night, at the far end of the deck, in intimate company with each other, gazing at the two corpses below. Neither shivered. Neither showed a sign of cold.

"It's rising at his cheekbones like the quiet sea—sinking him."

"Or like mother's love?" asked Agatha.

"Or like mother's comfort, mother's love, the cool white quilt. His hair has caught the powder. His beard is white—"

"As though he were too soon too old, and suddenly wise."

"Suddenly wise. Oh, Agatha, what a price to pay for wisdom. He looks like he's drowning without complaint. His nose and his forehead are a portrait framed in snow. He's sinking, sinking."

"Shirley, dear, do you feel like crying, now?"

"The drift has become his shroud. This mountain is his grave. I can't see him any more. He is sunken in the snow. God, how I wish he had been this wise and this quiet when he was alive. Agatha?"

"Yes, dear."

"I feel like crying now."

"The snow is surcease and forgetting," said Agatha. "Do, Shirley. Do cry now."

So the younger woman put her head on the older woman's shoulder and wept. Not a sound. Not a sob. Silent tears ran down from open eyes.

Chapter 4

NIGHT OF THE LIVING DEAD

STEPHEN R. LAWHEAD

"Hey, Stevens! A word."

Arthur Stevens turned and peered blearily into the countrified countenance of Wesley Willer. "In my experience," Stevens muttered, "people who want only a word never stop with one."

"I've seen you around and I've been meaning to introduce myself."

"See?"

"What was that?"

"You were saying?"

"We should get to know each other."

"Why?"

"Well, shoot, we're practically neighbors, you know. I have a feeling we could be real good buds. After all, we're both writers. I even wrote a fantasy book once. Sold about a million copies."

"Can I go?"

"Well, now that you mention it, some of us were wondering—don't take this the wrong way, it's nothing personal—but how should I put this? You knew Yates pretty well, didn't you?"

"I knew him."

"Well enough to kill him?" Hastings coasted up, hands stuffed in his pockets. "Nothing personal."

"Mind if I punch you in the nose? Nothing personal."

"Violent temper," whispered Hastings to Willer. "Write that down."

"You two taking notes?" Stevens demanded.

"We're undertaking a little informal investigation of our own," Hastings explained. "It was Gloster's idea."

"This whole thing was Gloster's idea. I wouldn't be at all surprised if *he* did it. One of his adolescent power fantasies. He's probably journaling about it: Murder as an Aphrodisiac."

"Hey, that's good. I can use that." Hastings snatched the notebook from Willer and scribbled in it.

"Be my guest," yawned Stevens.

"Any idea who might have had a good reason to kill Yates?" wondered Willer. "Purely speculative. That's what you're good at, right? Using the ol' imagination, and all that?"

"Fantasy writers get no respect," muttered Stevens. "Here, write this down, too: No, I did not kill Yates."

At least, he thought to himself, *I don't think I did. I'm pretty sure I didn't. I would remember a thing like that. I mean, jet lag does strange things to your head, but let's get a grip here.*

Not that he didn't have it coming. If people knew what Yates was really like, no jury in the country could convict me. Maybe I did *kill him after all. I can't remember.*

Probably, I did.

What am I saying? I'm so tired, I don't know what I'm saying. Maybe I'm the one that's dead. That's it! I'm dead. I'm a zombie!

"Look," Stevens told them, "much as I have enjoyed this little chat, I've just survived a fourteen-hour flight in steerage, two murders, and come this close to being hugged by Wesley Willer *here.* I've got to get some sleep."

He turned and was about to stagger up to his room when Livingston Johns hove into view.

"A true meeting of the minds! How refreshing." Johns did not so much waddle as roll unsteadily toward them.

"You found the cooking sherry!" cried Hastings, desperation making his voice crack. "Give over!"

Johns smiled warily. "'I beg your pardon, sirrah.' *The Merry Wives of Windsor;* act four, scene six, verse twenty-eight. The Bard is divine, don't you think?"

"I prefer Bacchus," Hastings sniffed.

"What did he write?" wondered Willer.

"Philistines," sighed Johns, rolling his eyes in poetic forbearance.

"Did someone utter my name?" Philippa d'Esprit materialized in their midst, looking like a togaed senator in purple terrycloth robe. "I am expecting a *very* important phone call from my agent in New York. You can reach me in the pool."

"No," remarked Hastings. "I'd rather not."

"Gee, she has an *agent,*" gasped Willer.

"In New York," added Johns.

"And phone calls by the pool." Willer and Johns glanced enviously after her regally draped, rapidly retreating form.

"Her real estate agent, no doubt," Hastings informed them, swiveling around. "Good work, you let your suspect get away."

They turned to see that the brooding, disgruntled Stevens had indeed vanished.

"He won't go far," replied Willer. "I'm rooming with him. I'll keep an eye on him."

"Wasn't Yates in that suite, too?" S. J. Smith asked, having joined the group while they gawked after Philippa.

Ignoring Hastings, Willer answered, "Was and is. Yates's stuff is still in his room."

"Maybe we should have a little look-see," suggested Smith delicately. He had once edited a compendium of Dorothy L. Sayers's mystery stories and felt he knew the right way to go about crime detection. "Unless, that is, anyone has any objections."

"I object," said Hastings. "But then, I object to everything."

"I, for one, have always considered you most objectionable," quipped Smith.

"Abuse from a man with a hand-painted palm tree on his necktie!" whined Hastings.

"Count me out," said Johns, sauntering away. "I promised to give Miss French a private reading. She is so, ah, willing."

"I thought we were going to check out Yates's luggage for clues," Willer insisted.

"I'd rather check out Felicity French."

"Down, Hastings!" said Smith. "Well, fellows, it's onward and upward." He pushed them up the stairs and along the rough-beamed corridor to Yates's room.

The room, like all the others, was done up in Holiday Inn chic: fuzzy red-orange shag carpet, wood-grain formica furniture, plaster lamps bolted to the dressers, yellow chenille bedspreads, and an adjoining bathroom plastered floor to ceiling in beige tile with tiny lilacs on each one.

Nathaniel Yates, true to all appearances, had been a very tidy person. His matching Gucci Travelaire and Executone briefcase—bought at tremendous discount—lay neatly stacked at the foot of his bed.

"Do we really want to do this?" wondered Willer aloud. "I mean, really?"

"No," Hastings replied.

"Yes," said Smith. "It's the only way to find out anything. Like. . . ."

"Like what happens to bozos who tamper with evidence in a murder case," suggested Hastings helpfully.

"Like why Yates was killed."

"I think we should let the shepherd do his job," offered Willer.

"We'll just have a quick look." Smith pressed the latch of the briefcase. "It's locked."

"So much for the thrill of discovery," remarked Hastings.

"Now, let's try the suitcase," said Smith, setting the briefcase aside. He pulled the suitcase to the edge of the bed, thumbed its latch, which sprang instantly open, raised the lid, and began shifting the contents.

Hastings crowded forward. "What have we here? Just as I thought. Ol' Nate was holding out on us." He reached in and withdrew a bottle of cognac, Courvoisier. "Let's have a snort," he said, brandishing the bottle and licking his lips. "What do you say?"

"It could be poisoned," warned Willer.

Hastings frowned. "All right, just a small snort then."

"Willer might be right. This could be how Yates was murdered."

"Nope," interrupted a voice from the doorway. "*This* is how Yates was murdered."

"Adolphssohn!" squeaked Smith. "You nearly gave me a heart attack!"

"Yeah, you shouldn't go around sneaking up on people like that," said Willer.

"And you shouldn't be going through Yates's stuff like that," replied Adolphssohn. "Anyway, I found this behind the toilet."

"What is it?" Smith took up the small brown cylinder Adolphssohn proffered on his palm.

"Can you smoke it?" wondered Hastings.

"It's a pill bottle," said Willer.

"Bingo!" Adolphssohn took back the plastic container. "Sleeping pills. The prescription is made out to N. Yates: fifty pills, and it was renewed only a week ago."

"Where's the lid?" asked Smith.

"No lid."

"Where are the pills?" asked Willer.

"No pills."

"Where is the corkscrew?" asked Hastings, returning his attention to Yates's luggage and a bottle of unopened wine just discovered.

"We should show this to the shepherd," suggested Adolphssohn. "This could be—"

What it could have been they would never know. For at that moment the genial give and take of civilized conversation was curtailed by a scream that could have curdled custard.

Out of the room, back through the corridor, and down the stairs they flew to find Agatha Gaines standing in the lobby, a limp piece of soggy paper dripping in her hand.

Adolphssohn was first to reach her. "Agatha, what is it? Were you attacked?"

"No, I. . . ."

Smith snatched the paper from her hand.

"What's this?" he demanded, holding the wrinkled paper at a distance for reading. "A note from the killer?"

"Amazing!" cried Hastings, scanning the page. "It's unintelligible. Absolutely incoherent. The fiend who wrote this must be utterly and completely psycho."

"*I* wrote that," sneered Agatha. "It's a poem."

"No wonder you screamed," sympathized Hastings.

Adolphssohn and Smith looked at each other and then at Hastings: "Shut up!"

"Nathaniel's body is missing," Agatha told them, grabbing back her poem. "I was writing an elegy for him, and I got to the part about pearly gates and all of a sudden was stumped. So I thought I'd go outside and look at his body—for inspiration, you see. Well, I went out and looked, and he wasn't there! He's gone!"

"Ooooee," shrieked Hastings, "it's *Night of the Living Dead!*"

"What do you mean by *gone,* exactly?" asked Smith, donning his best Lord Peter Wimsey manner.

"I mean *gone*—as in disappeared, vanished, nonexistent, lost to sight, seen no more, retired from view, where eyes may not follow. . . ."

"All right, all right," Adolphssohn soothed, "we get the idea."

"Now," said Smith, "think very carefully. What did you see? Details, we want details. Even the tiniest thing might be important. Now, what did you see?"

"Snow," replied Agatha. "Lots of snow, and Natesie's chair empty."

"Were there footprints?"

"I don't know."

"Was Rivers still there?"

"I didn't notice."

"You're a poet, for Heaven's sake! You must have observed something!" Smith exploded in exasperation. Wimsey never had it this rough.

"There's a blizzard out there! I noticed that. Look at me, I'm soaked to the bone."

"Oh, Agatha, if anybody ever needed a hug," Willer began, but—"Ooooff!"—he subsided when Shirley Kerns's elbow reached his rib cage, for a crowd had gathered.

"Let me get this straight," put in Adolphssohn. "You went outside in a blizzard to view Yates's body for inspiration and saw that his chair on the porch was empty, so you ran back in here and screamed."

"Precisely."

"We've got to confirm this," announced Smith. "There might be clues left behind. Who's going out with me?"

"Well, I'd rather not," snapped Agatha frostily. "It's cold out there. I'll catch my death."

"What about the rest of you? Is anybody going outside with me?" demanded Smith. The others shuffled their feet, trying hard to think of pressing engagements elsewhere. "Well?"

"Don't look at me," cried Hastings. "Nature gives me the willies!"

"Humpph!" sniffed Smith. "I shall go alone." He stomped off to find something to go over his sport coat.

"Maybe someone should go with him," Adolphssohn said, gazing after Smith. He paused thoughtfully, and added, "Just in case."

It was then that the lights went off.

Chapter 5

THE POOL

MADELEINE L'ENGLE

Philippa d'Esprit fled to the pool. There was too much noise, too much talking, too much death. Philippa and Agatha Gaines were rooming together. They were both recently widowed. These two subsequent irrational deaths shook them deeply.

Shirley Kerns and Lynne Teal had the adjoining room, and all four women shared the bathroom. One bathroom, with one wash basin, for four women, some of whom had the clutter of contact lens cases and fluids; others had hair curlers, bottles of lotion. Obviously this bathroom had been set up by men, or a man. Men had simpler needs.

They had been told by the odd deputy sheriff, the shepherd, to go to bed and to sleep, but how could anyone sleep with two dead bodies out in the snow and a blizzard howling around the building, shaking the old timbers? No, sleep was not possible.

Agatha was in the large meeting room, by the dying embers of the fire, pad and pen in hand, writing. She had pulled her privacy around her like a winding sheet. Philippa moved as quietly as possible to the pool, bumping into and almost overturning a chair. Righting it, she continued. In the pool room it was steamy, and the water was warm, too warm for real swimming. She tested the hot tub, and the water felt ready to boil. She took off her terrycloth robe and, sliding into the warm water of the pool, swam several laps.

"YOU!" a voice boomed.

Startled, Philippa looked up to see an enormous woman with Balkan features swaddled in a voluminous fur coat, several sizes too large. The long sleeves hid her hands. Fur dragged on the floor, hiding her feet.

"YOU!" she boomed again.

"Who are you?" Philippa demanded.

"Nemesis."

"What is your *name*?"

"I just told you," the woman said. She had an odd inflection, a slightly choppy accent. "Emma Syss. So. You are one of them writers."

"I am a writer, yes. Who are you, Ms. Syss, and what are you doing here?"

"Call me Em. You recognize my name?"

"Well. . . ."

"My books sell. Ask any Christian bookstore. I have true knowledge. I know when someone is a Christian and when someone is not. You are not."

Philippa remembered a book Agatha had once shown her, a book listing half of those present at Christhaven as being Communists or Satan worshipers. She asked, "Is—was Nathaniel Yates a Christian?"

The large woman shuddered. "No, he was not. God may, if he so chooses, rest his soul. But I doubt it."

"I still don't know why you're here," Philippa said.

"I ought to be here. It is my right. That Gloster should have invited me. I am a true Christian writer."

At that moment a scream pierced the air.

"Ah!" said Emma Syss. "Perhaps another one has met an appropriate end."

Philippa pulled herself out of the pool. "You horrify me."

"Why? Because I am of the true faith? Because those who are impostors will be struck down by the Lord's wrath?"

The lights flickered and went out. Philippa slid back into the pool. For the moment it seemed the safest place to escape

Emma Syss. Although, if Emma Syss could see her, she might well try to drown her.

"There is no safe place," came a man's voice.

Slowly Philippa's eyes adjusted to the white light coming into the room from the snow. A shadowy man's form was outlined dimly. Dolph Adolphssohn.

"Who is in here?" he asked.

"I am. Philippa. And Ms. Emma Syss."

"Good Lord," Adolphssohn exclaimed. "What on earth is she doing here?"

"Pointing her finger at most of us, including Yates, as not being Christian."

"Where is she?"

Philippa squinted against the strange white light. There was no large body in equally large fur coat. "She was here a moment ago."

"Philippa, are you hallucinating?"

"Certainly not!"

"Philippa, George Gloster would never have invited her."

"Of course he wouldn't," Philippa said. "She knows that, and she's angry at not being invited. That's why she's here." Despite the hothouse warmth of the room, she shivered.

Adolphssohn handed her the purple terrycloth robe; in the strange snow light it looked black. "Put it on," he ordered. "Then I think you'd better go to bed."

"You don't believe me."

"Philippa, my dear, if Emma Syss is in this place, surely someone else would have noticed her."

In the lobby light flickered. More light. Candles were being lit.

"Come," Dolph said gently.

"Dolph," Philippa said. "Emma Syss is *not* a figment of my imagination."

Philippa followed him toward the sofas. Someone had built up the fire, and the other members of the group were gathered there, Agatha sitting on the couch as though her legs would not hold her up, Shirley perched on the arm of a chair. Magdalene stood staring into the fire, her arms wrapped around herself as though in protection against the cold, and against the nervous stares of the others.

"Yates is gone," Agatha whispered. "He—is—gone."

S. J. Smith confirmed this. "But Rivers is still there, sitting in the chair. Yates's chair was overturned. And there was no body."

"Does—did Rivers publish Emma Syss?" Philippa asked the group at large.

"I believe so," Livingston Johns nodded.

"What does that have to do with anything?" Wesley Willer demanded. "He published several of my books, too. He was a good man, a good man."

"Why on earth, or Heaven," demanded Harold Hastings, "bring Syss up at this time and place?"

"Because she's here," Philippa stated flatly.

"Philippa, please," Adolphssohn said. "You're tired. You obviously have jet lag. You're in a state of shock."

"Emma Syss was in the pool room," Philippa protested, a shade too hotly.

Magdalene turned away from the fire. "She hates all Catholics. To her we're not Christians."

"Who *is* Christian, to her?" demanded Smith.

"Rivers, for one," Willer said. "Philippa, are you sure?"

She moved toward him, and he pulled her to him in a hug. "Thanks, dear Wes, for not thinking I've gone round the bend. I know I saw her."

Willer, his arm still protectingly around Philippa, said to the others, "I've known Philippa for a long time. While on occasion she does tend to overreact, she does not hallucinate."

Arthur Stevens murmured, "For hallucinations I came half way around the world to this. If she is jet lagged, what do you think I am?"

Shirley's bright hair gleamed gold in the candle light. A small smile touched her lips. "If—and I emphasize if—Philippa is by some strange chance right, and if by some strange chance Emma Syss is here, perhaps—just perhaps—we have found our murderer."

"Wishful thinking." Adolphssohn's voice was hard. "Scapegoating. We cannot eliminate the possibility that there is murder in the hearts of some of us. Or that this murder has been translated into an act. The fall is closer to us in time than we recognize."

Smith crossed to the windows and peered out onto the deck. "Still no Yates. Rivers is still there."

Gloster demanded, "Where's George Bent? Hasn't he been deputed by the sheriff?"

"And where else would I be but looking and listening?" a voice came from above, and they looked up and saw George Bent standing on the balcony, looking down on them. "Who's this alleged Emma Syss?"

"A sort of writer," Gloster answered.

"A published writer," Willer said.

Stevens said, "She approves of you. I'm not sure what that does for you in my estimation."

"Where is she?" Bent asked.

All of the assembled writers were looking up at the man on the balcony. No one saw the large body of a woman in an enormous fur coat cross the lobby and enter the pool room.

"I think she lives in Wheaton," Agatha said.

"Ah," Magdalene murmured.

"Remember," Agatha pointed out, "that the Theosophical Society is in Wheaton, too. Don't go jumping to conclusions."

"Are we," Lynne asked, "going to spend the rest of the night here? Or should we, perhaps, take candles and go to our rooms?"

"There's little left of the night," Stevens said, looking pointedly at his elaborate wristwatch.

"I note that Felicity is in bed and asleep," Gloster remarked.

"Well, she's not here," Shirley said. "I hope she's all right."

"Should we check on her?" Agatha suggested.

"It might be wise," Gloster nodded, "since it's possible that someone has already attempted to. . . ."

"Oh!" Agatha exclaimed. "Please do go, George."

"No, no," Gloster demurred. "It should be one of the women."

Magdalene asked, "Do you know what room number she's in?"

"Two, I believe," Gloster said. "It's downstairs."

"I'll go look, then," Magdalene said, "if someone will come with me. Shirley?"

"Why not?" Shirley shrugged. "It's better than sitting here, wondering, wondering. . . ."

The two women each took a candle and walked away, close together.

"So any one of you could have done him in." They all jumped, as Bent walked toward them.

"Or the apocryphal Ms. Syss," Hastings murmured.

"Apocalyptic," Stevens said.

"Apophatic," added Smith.

Willer looked directly at Bent. "I cannot have it in me to believe, I cannot have it in my heart to believe, that any one of us, called here together by George Gloster, could kill. We may all, as Dolph knows, have evil thoughts in our hearts, even murderous thoughts, but unlike those in the secular world, we do not believe in acting them out. We are not secular humanists, we are—"

He broke off as Magdalene and Shirley returned, Felicity between them. She held her wrists out in front of her stiffly. There was a deep mark across her mouth.

"She was in her room all right," Shirley said.

"Bound and gagged," Magdalene finished.

"But who?" Willer demanded. "Did you see who?"

Felicity sagged into a chair, shaking her head negatively. "The lights had gone out. I was reading, trying to calm myself, when the lights went out. I heard my door being pushed open," she shuddered, "and I heard someone coming toward me. I tried to scream, but my throat was closed with terror. Then someone grabbed me. Someone large, I know that, it was someone large. And furry."

"Emma Syss!" Philippa cried.

"I think we should pray," Felicity said. "Please do let us pray."

"Wesley?" Gloster suggested.

Willer demurred. "No, George. You are the one to lead us."

Adolphssohn nodded. "Pray for our souls, and the souls of Yates and Rivers. Pray for Philippa that she. . . ."

"Emma Syss is here." Philippa's voice rose slightly.

"Hush," Willer hugged her. "I believe you."

"Maybe coffee would help," Felicity suggested.

"Ah, coffee!" Dolph said. "Would that be possible?"

"The cook went home for the night. Bent let her go."

"In this storm?"

"She lives just at the end of the road. So she used snowshoes. We're used to snow up here."

"No coffee, then?"

"Couldn't we make it?" Shirley suggested.

"Maybe I could," Felicity said. "But I think we should pray first. Please."

Gloster glanced upward. Bent had returned to the balcony and was looking down on them. Gloster looked down at his clasped hands. "Dear Lord, . . ." he started.

"Good God!" It was Smith, who was peering out onto the deck, his hands cupped about his eyes so that he could see better.

"What?" Adolphssohn asked.

"Wait." Smitty's voice was low. He slid open the door to the deck and beckoned. "George!"

Cold air and snow rushed into the room. Gloster followed him, made a low murmur of alarm, a peal for Heavenly help.

Adolphssohn and Willer hurried after them, and the others, too, hurried toward the door that led onto the deck.

Yates's chair was still overturned, empty. Rivers's chair was there, and Rivers was sitting in it. But not as he had been when he had been placed there. Now he was swathed in an enormous fur coat.

Chapter 6

IN THE WOMEN'S ROOM

KAREN BURTON MAINS

"'Woman is woman's greatest ally,'" quoted Philippa d'Esprit. It was one o'clock, and she was standing at the entrance to the women's suite, an Artemisia ruling the upper level lodge, light from fireplace and hall casting upon her face and gown harlequin sequences of shades and shadows. "Euripides."

From behind her, commotion sounded; bumping, scraping—Lynne Teal's squeaky voice in command. Murder! Mayhem! She could stay silent no longer. Only writers—esoteric, impractical—would tolerate such a muddle. No one but she had thought to protect the women. She emerged from the room after an extended consultation, pushed past the older woman, and, leaning over the second floor balcony, called, "Gloster! Gloster!"

Teal's boss, meditating in front of the stoked fire, did not hear her at first; he was seeking, not without difficulty, the inner guidance of quietude. His dream for changing Evangelical publishing was being sabotaged. Bodies. Strange fat women. A detective trapper with bent syntax. Who was leading them all through this *danse macabre?*

He had attempted the prone meditative position, his nose mashed into the ash-flecked rug before the fieldstone fireplace; and while that distinguished his spiritual attitude, it had left his backside physically unprotected. Now he was sitting cross-legged, in contemplation, breathing deeply, diaphragm in—*wjooooo;* diaphragm out—*jhooooo. Wjooooo/jhooooo.* His spine, turned to the blaze, was being comfortably warmed. . . .

"Gloster!" Lynne's demand finally arrested his attention.

"Murder! Murder!" shouted a man's voice from behind a door on the second floor—Livingston Johns, an eloquent somniloquist, breathing lines from beneath cement-lidded slumber—"'sleep no more . . . pluck out my eyes . . . the multitudinous seas incarnadine. . . .'"

Oh help, thought Lynne, having never slept in company with so many writers; *they even dream in Shakespeare.* The creative mind was fine in small doses (very small doses), but desperate moments like these called for brilliant pragmatists—like herself. She had a plan.

By this time, the other authors, having risked murder in their beds, and now wakened by the cries "Gloster!" and "Murder!" were gathering.

"Yes," pronounced Philippa, her shadow looming imperious and august, "we the women have decided." Organ bellows filled her alto tones.

"Decided what?" Gloster was halfway up the stairs, his face still bearing the squash marks of pronal meditation.

Shirley pushed her way through the doorway of the women's room, past the other female forms. She was wearing bulky sweats, night cream, and curlers, and she looked the very paradigm of ordinariness.

"What an unhuggable apparition," whispered Willer to Magdalene, who appeared soft in doe-shaded velour, her brown hair snooded, hedged around by the embrace of her husband, S. J.

"Uncharitable," said the saintly Magdalene, who would never stoop to demean another woman's night attire.

"I heard that," said Shirley to Willer, deliberately cuddling him and messing her night cream across his whiskers.

"Most ungallant, don't you think, Magdalene?"

"You must understand, Wesley, that I am the reason my husband believes in God," said Shirley, who also smelled of Vicks Vap-o-Rub. "He swears a miracle occurs in our bathroom every morning between six and seven; each day I am utterly metamorphosed."

"'And must they all be hanged,'" intoned the sleeping Johns sonorously, melodramatically, "'that swear and lie?'"

"Wake that impractical lunatic," fired Lynne at Gloster, "and find Stephens." She took command. Organizational authority empowered her; practical mental powers gave her daring to face down the assembled literary *personae.* This must be done now, this next, and then this. "The women must be protected. We have decided to all sleep in the three-bed room. Consequently, we need you men to move the two beds out of the two-bed room now occupied by Philippa and Agatha into the three-bed room, which will be slept in by Philippa and Agatha, Shirley, myself, and Felicity. Felicity is now in the three-bed room. This means the women will become one another's protectors."

"Except for you, Magdalene," added Philippa. "We thought that you would prefer the embrace of your own husband."

"If you feel that you can trust him," said Lynne. "Otherwise, you are welcome to come with us."

Dazed by the forcefulness of Lynne's command, more used to indeterminate discussions like "The Esthetic of Christian Writing," the men moved instantly into action. Into the two-bed room they marched, Adolphssohn stripping sheets, blankets, stacking pillows; Willer and Hastings hoisting box springs and mattresses; Smith and Johns breaking down the headboards, sideboards, and slats.

In the three-bed room, Felicity was already tucked safely into the far bed by the window. She wore her lavender sweater for sleep, and she waggled her fingers flirtatiously when Johns, still slow and somnambulant, shoved beds one and two close, reassembled bed three from the other room and mis takenly attached the headboard to the foot end and the footboard to the head end, creating an awkward disruption in the symmetrical continuum of beds.

Agatha Gaines was already propped up in the next bed, cheerfully being game about the repositioning of furniture and the inconveniences it was causing. She had decided to journal the whole Christhaven experience; one so rarely consumed such an opportune conjuncture of emotion and event—terror, confusion, anguish, pathos, violence! Hoping she could do justice to this carnage, she had already filled forty pages in her cloth-bound notebook. Her negligee was made of sheerest brushed flannel, carmine. Her gray hair, which she had let grow long since her husband's death, fell stylishly and blended with the cowl of her blue fox coat, which she had placed around her shoulders for modesty. She lifted her head when the men entered the room, interrupted in her attempt to finish a kyrielle, struggling with the eighth syllable in the second quatrain—"A puff of the wind, life is ended"; no, "A puff of the wind, life is *out*"—and inspected each male carefully through gold-rimmed lorgnettes.

Philippa was directing the making of the beds. The strawberry and cinnamon plaid bedspreads with their matching pink sheets from the three-bed room had remained on the three beds nearest the window against the west wall. The aquamarine and chocolate plaid spreads with their matching beige sheets from the two-bed room were reassembled on the two beds nearest the door to the hall against the east end of the room. One pillow for each woman's head—one, two, three, four, five. Then, seeing that five beds crowded the three-bed room, she ordered them all to be pushed tightly together.

Awkward contingencies, these, but then one didn't deal with murder during ordinary writers' conventions; character slander perhaps, but not strangulation, poisoning, corpses.

If the beds weren't pushed together, no one could open the door to the bathroom. In fact, with the other articles of furniture in the room, there was now only a narrow passage between them and the walls. To get out, they would have to crawl over the footboards or over the sleeping forms of each other.

Shirley was to sleep in the middle bed—the one Johns had unfortunately reassembled hind end to. Philippa would sleep in bed two; Lynne in bed one by the door.

"This is not simply a repositioning, George—it's part of my master plan," the efficient assistant explained to her boss. "Every half hour the women will advance right one bed. For example, at the next shift, Felicity will move from the fifth bed at the far west window end to the first bed at the door at the east end. Agatha will advance one bed, from the fourth to the fifth, and so on, to morning. In that fashion, when a woman reaches the end position (by the windows), she knows that on the next move, she can use the bathroom and get a drink of water before returning to the first bed by the door. She doesn't need to disturb the other women out of turn, unless she's desperate or suddenly sick; then she can crawl over the footboard. She will also be safely returned to the first bed before the others are fully asleep after each rotation. Moving over one bed won't wake them up much, and if someone doesn't return, a light sleeper will certainly sound the alarm."

"And I," said Agatha, closing her journal, the eighth syllable having been satisfactorily discovered, "have an interior clock. It adjusts even when I cross time zones. I shall wake the women at each half-hour mark."

"To kill one of us," said Philippa, taking off her golden slippers and making ready to retire in the second bed, "the cold-blooded maniac will have to find her first. Otherwise, he'll have to murder us all. Highly unlikely," she said, slipping under the covers, "don't you think?"

Gloster looked into the women's room and smiled at the organizational genius of his assistant. Lynne smiled thinly in return, but a careful observer would have noted that the fleeting expression never softened her eyes.

"After the women are in their appointed beds," said Lynne to Gloster, "wait in the adjoining hall while Philippa reads compline. Then turn off the light, leave the door open a crack, press the snap lock, and close the outer door to the suite. We will all see you in the morning . . . that is to say, if we're still alive. I hope you men fare as well."

Shirley climbed into the middle bed, bed three, hurting herself on the misplaced headboard. She punched the pillow. Drat! It was too hard. Then she remembered she would be here only for the next half hour. Maybe she could find a compatible pillow and take it along on the rotation.

"Can't we choose a pillow that suits us?" she inquired, settling down under the strawberry and cinnamon plaid bedspread. The stern grimace on Lynne's face forbade any more such frivolous suggestions. This was a life-and-death matter.

"The Lord Almighty grant us a peaceful night and perfect end," began Philippa. Gloster waited outside the bedroom door for her to finish the office of compline, prayers that complete the day. The gentleness of her voice touched him as she intoned the final phrases, ". . . that awake we may watch with Christ, and asleep we may rest in peace." He heard the other women say the amen, Lynne's voice a tone louder than the rest, since she rested in the bed nearest the door. Whispering amen himself, and surprised by the emotion in the word—*so be it*—he pronounced the blessings on humans sharing common danger, turned the lights off, and shut the door . . . but he neglected to snap the lock.

For that hour Christhaven slept, while the winter wind sang its erratic cadence, dimmed by the drumskin of snow muffling the world before awakening.

Shirley was now in the fifth bed by the windows. The women had rotated twice; Philippa was in bed four, Lynne in bed three, Felicity in bed two, Agatha in bed one—by the door. Shirley kept counting the moving lumps—all safe so far, all breathing. Every cough, every wheeze, every rustle kept her awake. She had had her good cry, and tears still pushed her eyes each time she thought of the bodies on the deck. She pulled the silky edge of the blanket to her cheek in the comforting habit of childhood.

She'd lost her pillow in the first rotation, abandoning the hard one, but Felicity and Agatha had taken theirs along. Bed five, therefore, was pillowless, and now it was hot.

Five beds in a three-bed room; five women breathing the same closed air. She kicked her bare foot free of the sheets, pulled her sweat pants off, and wadded them beneath her head.

A noise from the empty room next door? A bumping, a shuffling of shoes across the floor? She tensed. She listened. Silence. She breathed. Nerves.

"Rotation," announced Agatha's weary voice from bed number one.

At least I can go to the bathroom, thought Shirley, *take some aspirin, cool my face.* Then she thought of the noises. Real or imagined? She crawled out of bed five by the window, fumbled her way down the line of footboards, headboard, footboards. She stubbed a toe and moaned aloud.

"Are you all right?" asked someone huskily.

"All right," Shirley replied. Foregoing the bathroom, she climbed into bed number one, fumbled for the sheet; it had become twisted beneath the spread and seemed to be tangled, a cat's cradle, knotted into the covers on bed number two.

She drowsed and woke, startled by a cough. A man's cough? Back to sleep. Awakened again. The occupant in bed number four seemed to be moving too much. Who was in bed number four? Agatha, Felicity, *Lynne?* Lynne was in bed number four. By the faint light Shirley watched the lump that was Lynne crawling over the footboard. "What's wrong?" she whispered, trying not to wake the other women.

Lynne scooched toward bed number one. "I have to go to the bathroom. I can't wait. And I can't sleep on the left side of the bed. I always sleep on the right. And that bed doesn't have a pillow. We started with five pillows. Where did they go?"

"I think just one is missing—on the floor maybe," whispered Shirley. "Why don't you sleep here? I'll get back into your bed." The bathroom door cracked open, and Shirley squeezed to the footboard of bed four, crawled over carefully, attempting not to disturb the sleeping partners on either side, Philippa in bed five and Felicity in bed three. It was only when she stretched out that she realized that Lynne had gone to the bathroom draped in the bedcovers.

Shirley was losing track. In which bed had she left her sweats? Hot as she was, she'd soon freeze without some covering. Carefully, she felt for the covers of the woman next to her. Philippa—surely a mother and a great-grandmother—would understand. The wind outside moaned, and Shirley thought of Whitewater and Nathaniel. She began to shiver. Death was blowing. And where was Lynne? What could be taking her so long?

Pulling gently, Shirley loosed the bedspread tucked beneath the form of Philippa. From bed two, Agatha started to snore. Was this the chocolate and aquamarine plaid or the strawberry and cinnamon plaid? Who cared? Her thoughts turned in weary cycle. Or was it the strawberry and chocolate?

From the bathroom she could hear muffled sobs. *We all find a personal place to cry. At least grief denotes life.* The sounds quieted eventually. The door cracked, light fell upon the beds, and Lynne crawled cautiously into bed number one.

Shirley didn't ask for the blankets belonging to bed four, not wanting Lynne to know she'd been heard weeping. Such a proficient little thing, why upset her any more?

"Who is in my bed?" yawned Philippa grandly, out of her sleep.

"Just me, just Shirley."

With that Philippa turned, whipping the hard-hoarded edge of covering off her bed companion.

Resigned, Shirley turned on her stomach, her arms tucked under her body, right leg kicking the bed rhythmically from the knee, another sleep habit from childhood. Bed number four grew wide in the night, vast and cold. Philippa turned in bed five, her pillow slipping between cracks. A pillow? Shirley swiped it shamelessly. Small comforts.

Did the lost boys in Peter Pan turn in bed on cue? she wondered. Relax head . . . relax forehead . . . relax eyebrows . . . relax . . . *or was it the five little Peppers?*

Another movement startled her. She sat up suddenly, stifling a scream. Someone was crawling into the middle bed next to her, but who was in bed three? Philippa, Lynne, Agatha, *Felicity?* Someone was trying to get Felicity. No, no, wait. It *was* Felicity. She was trying to get out, but because of Johns's fumbled handiwork, she was attempting to crawl over the headboard instead of the footboard, and she seemed suspended, strained at the top.

"Felicity? Felicity? Are you awake?" asked Shirley *sotto voce.* "Try the other end. Bed three is all mixed up, remember?" Leaning forward on her knees, Shirley managed to steer the flounderer from the headboard to the footboard end.

"Who is in my bed?" inquired the sleep-drugged voice of Philippa again.

"It's just us, Philippa," answered Shirley. "Felicity and Shirley, and we're not in your bed."

The bathroom door cracked wide, then closed all the way with a slam. "Psst. Psst," said a voice from bed one, "leave the door open." Lynne still in control.

"Rotation," announced Agatha, performing her responsibility somehow from the remote depths of sleep. Counting bodies, Shirley thought she reached five, including herself, but how could that be? Felicity had gone to the bathroom. Again: one, two, three, four, five. Sleep starved, Shirley shook her head. Blankets, clumps of tossed pillows. Her mind had become scrambled.

It was then, during rotation, as the women were all rolling over one bed to the right, that Shirley shamelessly grabbed the pillow from her bed four, yanked the bedcovers from bed number five, and plopped to the floor, rolling beneath a bedframe. *Oh, the bliss of warmth!* sighed Shirley to herself, plumping the pillow beneath her head. Tucking in the pink picks to her brush curlers that had become loosened in this rowdy night, she wrapped the covers cocoonlike around herself, keeping the silky blanket edge by her cheek. . . .

Felicity turned the bathroom light off, opened the door, and made her way safely to bed number three, unaware that another rotation had occurred. Oriented now, the Christhaven hostess clambered over the footboard with a little dive to land on the sleeping body of Agatha in bed number three. *Umph!* Felicity belonged in bed number four; maybe she would discover five was empty, maybe someone would share bedclothes. . . .

Shirley heard the creak of spring and mattress above her. It must be three o'clock. She wondered which bedspread she had, chocolate or strawberry. Relax. She wondered who the murderer was among them? Man or woman? Relax. She wondered—and finally slept. She no longer heard the muffled groans.

Light began to creep into the women's room, muted, storm-blotted natural light. It was the beginning of day in the Colorado Rockies.

Shirley's consciousness thrust into wakefulness as she heard someone walking. She opened her eyes to see an ankle in a man's shoe by the side of bed number one. Dream or waking? She dozed again. A scream—Agatha's.

"She's gone! She's gone!"

The murderer is a man, thought Shirley, comatose.

"Where's Shirley?" screamed Agatha again. "She's gone! She's gone! One of the beds is empty!"

Am I dead? thought Shirley. *No, I'm just under the beds.* "I'm down here, Agatha. I'm sleeping beneath the beds."

By this time, Agatha's screams had roused the other occupants of Christhaven. A pounding insisted itself against the outer suite door. Philippa was calming the poetess. Felicity was peering under the bed, her body still on the upper mattresses, since there was no room on the floor for kneeling. Adolphssohn's voice, Hastings's too.

Shirley rolled to the crack between the west window wall and bed number five, her head emerging, her shoulders pushing up in the tight space. "I just couldn't sleep up there." She found her discarded sweat pants—someone had hung them on a bedpost—and pulled them on.

Consultation, decisions, morning work—the two east beds moved back to the empty room. The men bumping in the tightened space. *Thump.* "Pardon." The bathroom door opened, closed. *Pom.* Gloster's morning heartiness—"Ho! Ladies! and how was the sleeping?"—*a man so determinedly cheerful must have something to be determinedly cheerful against,* thought Shirley.

"My journal. Where did I put my journal?" Agatha rummaged under the pile of stripped bedclothes. Water in the bathroom. Lynne brushing teeth. More pounding on the door. *Bam! Bam!* The door closing. *Pom.*

"Morning prayers," said Philippa. "Morning prayers in the great room. Ten minutes!" Felicity's voice calling, "Breakfast in an hour!"

Dazed with fatigue, Shirley began sorting the bedclothes. She stacked pillows. There were six. Six? One, two, three, four, five, *six!* Three strawberry and cinnamon plaid bedspreads, three sets of pink sheets. She and Lynne made the three remaining beds, now separated. Two chocolate and aquamarine plaid bedspreads, two matching sheets—folded, piled, carried to the next room. Shirley stretched and yawned. "What a night. . . ."

"When did you leave the beds?" asked Agatha, glancing up from the journal in which she was writing furiously.

"Soon after Felicity tried to climb Mount Kilimanjaro."

"That's strange," said Agatha. "As a safety measure, I kept counting five bodies in the beds during every rotation. There were five bodies all night."

Shirley shrugged her shoulders—they couldn't even keep a pillow count, let alone a body count. Shirley waved her off, a helpless, no-use-explaining motion.

"Actually, I slept amazingly well," said Agatha. "Words from Whitman's *Reconciliation* wove like a thread through my dreams:

> Word over all, beautiful as the sky,
> Beautiful that war and all its deeds
> of carnage must in time be utterly lost,
> That the hands of the sisters Death
> and Night incessantly softly wash
> again, and ever again, this
> soil'd world. . . ."

Listening, Shirley suddenly remembered the contraband bedclothes she had warrened beneath bed number five by the window. She bent over to pull them out, stopped still, the fabrics dangling from her motionless hand. She and Lynne had made the beds. But this bedspread was yellow and apple green plaid. And these sheets were lime. What—?

Philippa opened the drapes and discovered to her dismay that it was not dawn but false dawn that had awakened them. It was too late to go back to bed even if the beds had remained as they were. A flurry of snow sifted through the outside air. The three women avoided glancing down toward the corner of the lower deck to check on the refrigerated body. The curtain's hem dangled across the orange shag of the rag carpet. A dark object rested where the drapery had hung.

It was a man's shoe.

Shirley looked at the poet. A question rose in both their eyes. Exactly who had been in bed with them that night in the women's room?

Chapter 7

THE BLUE TATTOO

CALVIN MILLER

It had been the rumor of Emma Syss's bizarre and snowy entrance to Christhaven that so troubled Stevens Thinking of her kept him turning between the sheets till 5 A.M. He could never sleep well while his mind was unsettled. Often it was thinking of a woman that roused him into his half-conscious duels with insomnia. More often his concern was measured in direct proportion to her bust line. He therefore felt odd, lying in a snowbound lodge, trapped between his insomnia and unfounded rumor, thinking about Ms. Syss. Not only was she flat in front, but her hair fell in Brillo pad curls, and her pudgy body was topped by a thick neck and her chinless head. She looked like a cruet of vinegar and was sexually remote—as cold as a fall onion.

He first met Emma at a Charismatic conference, where he had gone as a local news reporter to write a story on a prominent faith healer. They had a beer together and generally agreed that faith healers were "witching warts" and were being paid handsomely for it. Perched on a bar stool, she grew firm and shouted, "I would never have a thing to do with emotional religions!"

He knew she meant it, too.

Later, however, he read an article of hers in a religious magazine, saying that, after listening to an old PTL rerun, she had broken into glossolalia. Apparently she was as fickle as she was sexless.

Philippa secretly admired Ms. Syss. The question was, What on earth was Syss doing at Christhaven? Or was she really there? It suddenly struck Stevens that Philippa was the only one who had seen her, and there was some doubt in his mind that Philippa could be trusted. She had once won an important literary medal in England, it was true, but it was also true that the book was a fantasy novel. Of all novelists, Stevens felt, fantasy novelists were the last to be taken seriously.

His mind wandered from the elusive Emma Syss back to the corpses that now were the rigor mortis sentinels of this ghastly arctic night. Was there a thread that connected the murders of Rivers and Yates? He shuddered when he remembered that the Yates corpse had just up and disappeared into the felted silence of the falling snow. At least the fur-wrapped corpse of Rivers still sat staring out over the Rockies with ghastly, glazed eyes.

"Yates at the dinner table, Rivers in the tub," mused Stevens aloud in the loneliness of his room.

"Yates at the dinner table, Rivers in the tub," said someone, repeating his words like an unwelcome echo.

It was Adolphssohn, whom Willer of Wyoming liked to call "the writer of the rooster book." Adolphssohn also had won an important medal for his book, so it was not easy for Willer to pooh-pooh his achievement. Willer said he was not generally into rooster books, even award-winning rooster books. Secretly, though, Willer, like much of the literary world, was mad about this particular rooster book. It was sheer envy that caused *him* to be uncritical.

"*Adesne tuipse?*" asked Adolphssohn, who used a lot of Latin in his novels. "A denarius for your thoughts, Arthur."

"I was just thinking, Dolph. There has to be a common thread linking these two murders. They must have been done by the same hand, since it is unlikely that there could be two murderers here at Christhaven."

"Highly unlikely, Arthur, I agree."

The two men sat in silence, trying to think of a common link.

Looking far away, Stevens drummed his fingers on the table and started humming "Camelot." For seven years he had been working on a novel about King Arthur. It had been seven years of tribulation, and humming "Camelot" kept his sagging spirits from folding altogether. His humming, however, bothered the rooster novelist, since he detested all themes from pop musicals. "It's plain unnatural to hum 'Camelot' for seven years," he had once said to Willer. Besides, Willer, who was Stevens's roommate at Christhaven, discovered that the neo-Arthurian also wore leotards under his pajamas. Stevens's whole fragile psychology was sweltering under a Camelot complex. Most unwholesome! Willer even admitted, under pressure, that while he liked hugging most everybody, he drew the line at hugging anyone who had worn leotards and hummed "Camelot" for seven years.

Adolphssohn's hollow eye fixed on an icicle outside the window as his vacant stare grew mica. The brilliant Latin writer was as epileptic as Dostoevsky himself. But in a moment Stevens could see that it wasn't epilepsy. The quivering Germanic jaw was an indication that it was only catatonia and not death.

"Gallia est omnis divisa in partes tres," said the plastic-masked Adolphssohn. His catatonic state reflected old emerging Latin lessons ripping from his slack jaw and tongue. He continued on, leaving Caesar for Ovid, *"O soror, O conjunx, O femina sola superstes!"* His Latin delirium passing at last, he vaulted up excitedly, crying.

"My god, Stevens, *VIDEO NUNC!*"

"Video? Sweet Teresa, the video shacks are closed at this time of night."

"Not VEE-day-oh . . . WEE-day-oh! Now I see! What is the one thing that Yates and Rivers have in common? Yates dying *ante cenam* and Rivers *in balneo.*"

"I don't follow," said Stevens, his speaking interrupting his humming.

"Don't follow? It's bright as the *Stellae Arcturi!* Big as the *T* in Tintagel! Yates loved writing books on pain, and Rivers liked causing writers pain."

"Yes, but how does that track?"

"Don't you see that Philippa has been wearing those maternity dresses, *stolae matris,* if you will? It was at her insistence that Yates was seeking to have a book published called *It Hurts When It Hurts: A Guide for Christians with Arthritis.*"

"And Rivers rejected his manuscript."

"*Bingo, bingonis!*" cried Adolphssohn, as though *bingo* were a third declension noun.

"I can see that Yates might have had a motive, but Yates was murdered first."

"Yes, but he might have slipped a phial of *agua Lethaea* into his ditty bag."

"*Pax vobiscum,*" said Gloster approaching. It was he who, when something should have been done about those poor corpses in the snow, could only talk about remote spiritual things. Being in no mood for his infernal monkish nature at this time of night, Stevens and Adolphssohn clammed up. "What's the matter, Adolphssohn, cat got your *lingua?*"

"You might as well know we think we may be on to a double attempt at murder," said Adolphssohn.

"We know Yates resented Rivers, and Rivers Yates," said Stevens.

"We think they might have killed each other."

"Yates prearranged Rivers's death out of resentment because Rivers had refused to publish *It Hurts When It Hurts.* The motive is clear."

"I will not be disturbed." Gloster was on his way to early morning prayer and had no urge to get involved in murder motives. "I'm celebrating my spiritual discipline."

"Not again!" said Stevens.

"Your earmuffs look funny," said Adolphssohn. "They muff on only one side."

"I change the muff from side to side as the exposed ear gets cold. It's simple and at the same time it's austere. And it keeps me from getting used to the luxury of double muffs. Simplicity ever seeks self-denial."

"*Sancta simplicitas!*" muttered Adolphssohn as Gloster walked away.

"Oh, by the way," said Gloster, popping back into the room, "you might be interested to know that late last night I saw Willer and d'Esprit hugging in the pool. And talking to them was a strange woman who is not part of our colloquium. *Pater noster, miserere mei,*" he whispered as he turned and left the room, "and bless my cold ear!"

"You still haven't made it clear how the double murder could have occurred," said Adolphssohn when Gloster had gone. "Wouldn't there had to have been an agent?"

It was a fair question, thought Stevens as he arrived at the bottom of the stairs and walked through the lobby toward the sliding doors. He peered out, examining the frozen face of Rivers through the distortion of ice crystals bonded to the window. Funny, there seemed to be a note attached to the collar of his big fur coat. Pushing the door open against the balking wind, he dashed barefoot the three or four steps toward the corpse and grabbed the note. The paper tore as the pin holding it did not give way.

"*Quid de notula?*" asked Adolphssohn. Stevens was unable to translate any Latin phrases beginning with *quid* and could not guess what the English was. But he closed the door, shutting the paralyzing air outside.

"It's a poem, I think," said Stevens.

"Lege."

"Hold your *equos,"* said Stevens, trying to prevent himself from punching the impertinent Adolphssohn right on his *nasonem.* Unfolded at last, it was indeed a poem, which Stevens attempted to read aloud:

> Seek the cause of dying in the ice,
> Hot as a penguin's foot in the epicore of Hell.
> Trust the Writer, not the Publisher,
> For Hemingway who's fishing is in another world now.
> Let it snow, let it snow, let it snow.

It was abstract, like all of Agatha's poetry, yet if it was her poetry, Stevens knew she had plagiarized the last line from Eydie Gormé.

"But let's not pass the possibility that Agatha is a suspect in the murders," said Adolphssohn.

"Along with d'Esprit and Willer in the pool. And don't forget Kerns and 'Society of Jesus' Smith," added Stevens. "For all I know, Adolphssohn, even thou art guilty."

"Et tu, Stevens? Ecce Homo homocidi!"

"What about Oklahoma City?" asked Stevens.

"I said *homocidi, HOMOCIDI,* not Oklahoma City!"

"Two to one, it was either Emma or Philippa or perhaps both. What could a Charismatic and an Episcopalian have in common? Only one thing. A repugnance for sniveling self-abuse titles like *It Hurts When It Hurts!"*

"Not bad," said Adolphssohn. "Syss would object on the basis that God can heal anything that is wrong with everyone and thus no one ever need be hurt."

"And Philippa?"

"Well, Philippa, being Episcopal, would prefer more elegant religious books rather than the kind Mr. Yates—or rather, the late Nathaniel Yates—wrote."

"Quick, let's to the pool and see if we can find some clues!"

Hurrying down the corridors, the two felt something Transylvanian about the Christian lodge. When they arrived at the pool and opened the foggy glass door, they found no evidence of the swimmers of the night before, neither Willer nor d'Esprit nor the elusive Ms. Syss. But there, floating pantless, face downward in the pool, was the ice blue form of Nathaniel Yates, thawing in the tepid water. Both knew it had to be Yates, for tattooed on his buttocks were the words *It Hurts When It Hurts.* The varicose derriere was now so blue that the blue of the tattooed letters, having receded into his water-wrinkled cellulite, were barely obvious. Still, the letters were there where the needles of any nurse might have once caused the living Yates considerable pain.

"Killed, frosted, thawed, and chlorinated all in a single night," muttered Stevens. "My God, Dolph, this whole tale makes Mary Shelley look like Dr. Seuss!"

"Shall we pull him out?"

"Let him float till the shepherd of Cripple Creek comes in to have a look."

"I've got to get some rest," said Adolphssohn, the fatigue of the night finally catching up with him. Stevens agreed, and they both retreated along the carpet where the path of snow cleats had long ago taken the richness from the pile. "Bolt your door, Arthur."

"You can bet on that!"

"Pax tecum."

"Oh, cut the Latin crap!"

Adolphssohn pulled into his room, stripped to his underwear, which was his usual nightwear, and climbed into bed. It was now 5:35 A.M., quiet as a Russian snowstorm and equally as ominous. "*Gallia est omnis divisa in partes tres. . . .*" He had not finished the prologue of *De bello Gallico* when he was sound asleep.

Haunted by connections that wouldn't connect, Stevens lay long awake. Who was shifting Yates from porch to snow to pool? Why was the corpse floating face downward, the telltale dorsal tattoo exposed for all to read? He began to rebuke himself for never having taken the time to read *It Hurts When It Hurts;* maybe the text itself held the clue to Rivers's animosity. And that verse of Agatha's—and was it really her verse? He had never been able to understand her poetry, although he had returned to it again and again, hoping that he might at least understand it if not like it. But her verse pinned to Rivers's coat remained as cryptic as the rest. . . .

Suddenly he sat up, remembering how he had once used his Sky King ring to unscramble cereal codes in the early fifties. If he took the word opening and closing each line, he found that the message did make sense.

> SEEK the cause of dying IN THE ICE,
> Hot as a penguin's foot IN THE EPICORE OF HELL.
> Trust THE WRITER, NOT THE PUBLISHER,
> For Hemingway who's fishing IS IN ANOTHER
> WORLD NOW. . . .

Agatha too must have had a Sky King ring—Cereal Box 1952, Battle Creek, Michigan—and was dumbfounding the literary world with it.

Having exulted over his discovery, Stevens quickly quieted down to contemplate the dismal conundrum of horror that remained. "The Writer, not the Publisher, is in another world"; he uttered aloud the heavy words that cryptically implied only one of the two deaths, the Writer's, was real. . . .

Light struck all of a sudden! Stevens pulled on his mukluks and his parka and hurried downstairs and out onto the rotted and frozen sundeck. There sat the publisher. Rivers certainly looked dead, but as the frosty face turned slowly toward him, Stevens felt such a chill in his breast that an icicle might just as well have been plunged into his heart.

"Arthur, how sweet of you to come," purred Rivers, lashing out with his furry right arm, grasping Stevens as he attempted to draw back. "If there's anything I can't stand, it's books on Arthur of England."

"More than books like *It Hurts When It Hurts?*"

"Remember T. H. White's glorious tombstone, *Hic jacet Arthurus, Rex quondamque, Rex Futurus?* Stevens, I'm going to make you pay for prying old Arthur from his grave."

"But what about Agatha's poem? Was it a prophecy?"

"I knew that one day, if you kept trying, you would understand her verse. But I will not have you telling the world that the secret of her literary power is a Sky King decoder."

"Are you and Agatha in this together?" asked Stevens, trying to wrench free, but his feet could find no traction on the ice-covered balcony, made even more slippery by the still-falling snow. "Did the two of you hatch the murder of poor Yates?" He tried again to free himself, but it was no use. "I'm next, is that it?" he cried on his knees, bent double by the pain. "Has Aggie already written a verse of curse for me?"

Stevens felt himself slipping, and then his head struck something hard, and the warm red blood seemed to mat in his hair and stream across his face. . . .

He was growing unconscious, or was he? He fought to make sense of his last conscious light. *Who had brought Rivers a coat?*

Swimming in a coma now, he heard a woman's voice. Was it Agatha's or Philippa's? The woman who emerged in the dying light seemed to be wearing a baggy dress, but he couldn't be sure. Down, down, down went the volume of his soul's light until he was at last in icy darkness.

Was he falling, or was it just a sensation? Demonic dreams dragged him through a Technicolor delirium. He passed King Arthur and Adolphssohn playing Scrabble in Latin, while Ovid begged them to let him into the game. He saw Shirley MacLaine out on a limb, talking to Morgan la Fey. Then he passed Gloster with his right ear muffed, singing

Quaker hymns to Shirley Kerns as they leafed through old Tammy Bakker picture albums. . . .

Nothing made sense, except one thing: Willer was hugging Smitty's wife and saying, "Mag, do you think Livingston Johns wrote *Leviathan Blues* underwater?" The word *water* was significant in his delirium, for by sunrise, Nathaniel Yates was not the only floater in the Christhaven pool.

Chapter 8

NOTHING GOOD EVER COMES

ALICE SLAIKEU LAWHEAD

There was no snow in England that day; no white-capped mountains or distant horizons; no fur coats, mystery guests, or floating corpses. What there was was coal smoke, humidity, and yet more rain for Mrs. Arthur Stevens.

And the call: the sharp double ring, the incessant double ring coming from an archaic green bakelite telephone that made Mabel wish—for the seventeenth time that day—that she was back in the United States where plastic pastel instruments chirped, beeped, chimed such intrusions.

"Oxford 822689," she droned into the receiver. "May I help you?"

A faint beep, something that sounded like the rustling of papers, two clicks, static, and white noise: a trunk call. That would be Arthur, calling from Colorado to say that he had safely arrived, that he loved her, and to ask how were the kids, was there much traffic driving back from Heathrow. . . .

"Art?"

"Ma'am?"

"Art, is that you?"

"Ma'am, this is George Bent calling from Colorado. How are you doing this morning?"

"It's not morning here, Mr. Bent. It's three in the afternoon."

"This would be Mabel Stevens?"

"Yes, it's Mabel Stevens! What's happened to Art?"

"The worst possible thing has happened to your husband, ma'am. . . ." Static, other voices on other lines in the distant background, a delayed transmission.

Sod all, muttered Mabel to herself. *It had to be one of those wretched connections where the time delay has everybody talking on top of each other.*

"What? I can hardly understand you."

"I said, the worst possible thing has happened to Mr. Stevens, ma'am. He arrived at Christhaven lodge yesterday, but this morning he was found, face down and dead, in the swimming pool."

"Is this Eddie?"

"Ma'am?"

"You've gone too far this time, Ed."

"Ma'am, my name is George Bent. I'm sort of a shepherd in Colorado, near Christhaven, where they've got all these writers, you see. Well, at least two of them have died in the past twenty-four hours, and I'm here to investigate and just generally keep everything on an even keel until the snow stops and the authorities can get their cars started to do it all proper."

"How's Susan? How're the kids?" Well, it was good to hear from Ed even though his phone tricks were over the top. "Did Art call you, then?" She paused for the answer, hearing yet more interference on the line, more rattles and clicks, more white noise. Then there was another voice.

"Mabel, this is S. J. Smith. No doubt you remember me. We met last year at CBA."

And then it came. The pressure, the tremendous pressure squeezing her head into a too small space, pushing her chest hard against her lungs, making the beating of her heart a pounding blast in her ears, swelling her hands. . . .

"Mabel, this is S. J. Smith," repeated the voice. "Are you there, Mabel? Mabel, are you okay?"

"He's dead?"

"Yes, Mabel, your husband is dead."

"Are you certain? Maybe he's. . . ."

"I'm sorry, Mabel. Do you have someone there?"

"I'm in Oxford! No one lives in this bloody city! I'm all alone, aren't I? I have the boys. . . . Oh, Smitty, I'm all alone here, and I'm starting to talk like a Brit!" Air came into her burning lungs with great pain.

"Mabel, I'm going to turn the phone back to Mr. Bent. Everything's upset here too, and he needs to ask you some important questions. Are you okay, Mabel?"

"Yes, yes," she said, headache and nausea beginning to insinuate themselves.

"Can you answer some questions?"

"I think so."

"Remember, Mabel: *ad majorem Dei gloriam!*"

"Oh, don't be such an ass, Smitty! All that jesuitical stuff can't help me now!"

The clicks, the static, the return of the other voice.

"Mrs. Stevens? George Bent again. I'm going to ask you some questions, and the only reason I'm doing it is that there's no one else here I can trust. . . ."

"I told him no good would come of going to writers' conferences. I always told him, 'You can act like a writer, or you can write.' Buns up in a swimming pool, indeed. Just like him, really, to get himself killed in a fit of dramatic pique. Great stuff for a legend, but that man has two kids!"

"Mrs. Stevens, I need for you to stay calm, here."

"Maybe he's worth more dead than alive. Maybe that's what he was thinking of—letting death put new life into his backlist."

"You can go ahead and fall apart later. Have we got a deal?"

"But I've already fallen apart, Mr. Bent," she said as she sank to the floor by the phone.

"Now Mrs. Stevens, what was your husband's relationship to a Mr. Nathaniel Yates?"

"Nathaniel! Did Nathaniel kill Art?"

"I'm afraid that Nate Yates is dead too."

"Don't call him Nate. His friends don't call him Nate. Call him Nathaniel."

"Either way, ma'am, he's dead."

"What's the matter with you people? Has everyone gone mad?"

"That's exactly what we need to find out, Mabel."

"Get on with it."

"Can I call you Mabel?"

"Just get on with it."

"I'm going to run through the list of people who are here at Christhaven, Mabel, and then I'm going to ask you to tell me what you know about these folks, especially anything that might help us with this here problem that's been developing. . . ."

"With the murder, you mean?"

"Yes, ma'am, it looks like murder."

"Well, if Nathaniel wasn't dead, I'd say he killed Art. Did he die before or after Art?"

"Before."

"Farewell, the primary suspect."

"Why don't you go ahead and tell me what you know about him."

"Well, Nathaniel was Art's boss years ago, and we got to be really good friends with him and his wife. . . . Have you called Lynette?"

"Yes, ma'am, I've called her."

"Mind you, she'll have been well provided for. Cor! What's going to happen with Art's books? Who'll finish them? Seven years he's been searching for the Holy Grail—now what? I can't finish them, and wouldn't if I could. I'm sick and tired of tramping around Wales, ogling castle ruins and deserted Roman forts, slogging through all that Celtic miasma. Haven't I got books of my own to write? Of course, Dan—that's his editor—will want the advance back. Well, he can jolly well come and get it, can't he? He can jolly well come over here and help me pack up all our stuff and move back to Idaho and see how much money he finds left in the cookie jar!"

"Mabel, get hold of yourself!"

"'Publishers *are* all cohorts of the Devil; there must be a special Hell for them somewhere.' Goethe said that, Mr. Bent."

"This is a name I haven't heard before," said Bent. "Mabel, where can I get in touch with this Goethe person?"

"He's in Germany, and he's been dead for two hundred years."

"Well, that's one less suspect to worry about. Now what I want to know right now is why you think Yates would kill your husband."

"Let's just say he keeps—kept—long accounts. He'd been around, and he had more dirt on everybody than anybody."

"What dirt did he have on your husband?"

"Ask anybody about Art, Mr. Bent, and they'll all tell you the same thing: he doesn't disclose, doesn't open up—not to strangers, not to his friends, not even to his wife. He has a secret life—or at least he *had* a secret life, and it wouldn't surprise me if that was the death of him. Literally."

"What about this George Gloster fellow, the one who called the little group of geniuses together?"

"The man who writes a book about the evils of wealth, lust, and domination—and then publishes it in hardcover and graces the dust jacket with a picture of himself looking rich, sexy, and powerful? I've never met him."

"You seem to know an awful lot about him."

"'I never desire to converse with a man who has written more than he has read.'"

"Can I quote you on that, Mabel?"

"That's Samuel Johnson."

"Friend of yours?"

"Sure, but he's been dead for centuries, too."

"Harold Hastings, do you know him?"

"Only by reputation . . . friend of a friend. Very talented, if you like his sort of thing. That novel of his, *Bloody Fool,* made him quite the darling."

"Was that a murder mystery, Mabel?"

"I would have enjoyed it more if it had been."

"Is he a killer?"

"Only literarily speaking."

"Livingston Johns."

"Criminy! Is that randy old goat there? Guard your women tonight!"

"Ma'am?"

"He's a lady killer, if not a writer murderer. His list of debaucheries is longer than. . . . Let's just say, Mr. Bent, that he has this perverse philosophy of sin. For him the only mortal sin is plagiarism, because it murders one's essence. Everything else is venial, including adultery and fornication. He revels in those, a celebration of failure in which God's forgiveness and man's humanity are made manifest. Some such heresy. That's all a dodge, though."

"Mabel, are you sure all this is to the point?"

"'All a writer has to do is get a woman to say he's a writer; it's an aphrodisiac.' Saul Bellow."

"Bellow," echoed Bent, desperate for fresh leads and new suspects.

"Johns's pitiful literary efforts have kept him in a state of arousal for as long as I've known him. Mostly he hits on buxom coeds trapped in his writing classes, and aspiring Jungian poetesses. Of course, his affair with Magdalene Smith is legendary."

"Now she's here," said Bent, glad to hear a familiar name.

"Aha! There you have it, then. Magdalene Smith, of course. Now, she's got talent. She probably lobbied Gloster on Johns's behalf—so that he could come. What other reason could

George have had for inviting him? That man's a walking indecency. Not to mention indiscreet!"

"Indiscreet?"

"Just to give you an example of what I mean. Poor Smitty came across reams of tatty correspondence from Johns to Maggie—the cad kept copies of everything—but the real heartbreaker was her replies, all written in that affected calligraphic style of hers. Really, it was all too much. Smitty tried to make light of it, and it was pitiful. If he wasn't such a devoted Catholic, the shame of it would have stopped years ago. Serve Johns right, I say, if Smitty did set Maggie free—force the issue. *A bon chat, bon rat.*"

"If you say so, Mabel. Any connection between these people and your husband?"

"Art admired all three—artistically and personally. Don't ask me why. I could never stomach the lot."

"Let's keep going. Agatha Gaines."

"'Poets aren't very useful. Because they aren't consumeful or very produceful.'"

"Edgar Guest?"

"No, Ogden Nash."

"You sure do know who said what, Mabel."

"Don't mind me. It's an English conceit. I'll get over it, whee, once I get out of here—*if* I ever get out of here. Look, I don't know Agatha Gaines."

"Lynne Teale?"

"Who's she?"

"Gloster's assistant."

"Keep going."

"Felicity French?"

"Who *are* these people, Mr. Bent?"

"Felicity's the proprietor of Christhaven. Do you know Dolph Adolphssohn?"

"'I know only what I read in the papers.'"

"Will Rogers!"

"Good, Mr. Bent, good."

"So what do the papers say?"

"That he's a writer's writer. Everyone there wants to be like him when they grow up."

"Did your husband know him?"

"Why don't you ask? Oh, blast! I just remembered that he's dead. Is Art dead?"

"Yes, Mabel, he's still dead."

"How many more people are you going to ask me about? I think I'm beginning to lose it."

"Philippa d'Esprit?"

"Well, of course, she's the one, isn't she, the one they all went to see and admire. *Dark and Stormy Night* and all that. I remember reading that book years ago . . . but I've never met her, and I'm sure Art's never met her. Anyway, why would she kill Art? She'd just glide over him. What motive would she have?"

"Well, that's all the participants at the conference I can think of right now, but while you're on the line—and you're doing a dandy job, Mabel, just dandy—I have a couple of clues you might be able to help me with."

"Shoot. Oh, he wasn't shot, was he, Mr. Bent? He hated guns—we both did. Much better for him 'the dolorous stroke of the naked steel,' 'the Saxon's jagged blade.'"

"Well, it's interesting that you should mention that. He did get some sort of blade through the chest; maybe it went into his lungs or heart. It's hard to say. The blade wasn't jagged, though."

"Well, that's a relief."

"And we don't know how Yates died. But there was one strange thing. A metal plaque next to his body that said PERHAPS TODAY."

"Is that so?"

"The real interesting thing is, there was a lipstick smear over the word PERHAPS."

"That should be easy to trace."

"Fact of the matter is, Mabel, I'd value your opinion, as a woman, about something I came across today."

"What's that?"

"I've managed to search the luggage, purses, and pockets of everyone who is here at the lodge, and I've come up with a woman's case that seems to be missing something. Let me see, here's the list. Moss green eye shadow. Green kohl eye pencil. Something called 'Erase.' Dusty rose liquid foundation. Dusty rose pressed powder. 'Blush-On.' Brown-black mascara. And pressed eyebrow color, brown."

"Read the list again." As he recited the inventory a second time, she could see the contents as clearly as if they were being laid out on the floor in front of her. Something was indeed missing. "It's dead simple, Mr. Bent. No lipstick."

"I thought so."

"Any woman who wore that much makeup would wear lipstick too. Was all this stuff in her purse or her pocket?"

"It was in a small zippered bag inside her purse, but I searched the rest of her purse, and the pockets of her coat."

"Well, then, you've got a first-class clue on your hands, Mr. Bent."

"I'm glad to hear you figure it the same way."

Mabel was moving into high gear now. The missing lipstick had all but obliterated the reality of her husband's death, but Bent changed the subject.

"I forgot to ask you about Wesley Willer. What do you know about him?"

"Wesley lives near us, when we live in the States."

"Friend of yours?"

"Never met him."

"And last but not least, Whitewater Rivers."

"What's he doing there? He's not a writer—he's an editor!"

"The way I understand it, the company he works for put a mess of money into this little soiree, and that means he gets to sit in on the festivities, whether the rest of them like it or not."

"You know what they say, Mr. Bent. 'Every editor should have a pimp for an older brother so that he has someone to look up to.' I'd like to think that Rivers has such a brother—it would be so nice for him."

"Isn't that a little ungenerous?"

"As adulterous as Johns is, that's how covetous Rivers is. The man wants whatever and whoever belongs to someone else. It's an unquenchable lust for other publishers' writers. If I were you, I'd ask Mr. Rivers straightway who's publishing with him these days—and who isn't. The *isn't* will be the key."

"Good idea, Mabel, but the problem is, he's disappeared."

"Just what kind of place are you running there?"

"Fact is, we all figured he was dead. But it seems he's only missing. And the way things look, he seems to have left of his own accord."

"Could it be that Art isn't dead either? I'll bet Art isn't dead at all."

"Oh, he's dead all right, Mabel. Mabel? Can you stay with me just a little longer? You're doing a fine job, just fine. But I need to know more of what you can tell me. . . ."

Mabel had dropped the phone and left it dangling while she went to the sideboard and poured herself a tumblerful of anesthetic, good British gin; it was one of the few pleasures of living in Oxford.

"Mabel, Mabel, are you there?"

"I'm not good for much more, Mr. Bent," said the new widow when she picked up the phone with her free hand. "Hurry up and finish."

"Do you know Agatha Gaines, the poet lady?"

"I know she has green eyes, and I know she wears lipstick. . . ."

And with that the receiver of the phone became unbearably heavy in Mabel's hand. She allowed her arm to realize its full weight as she eased it away from her face and placed the receiver gently into the cradle. The phone gave a parting *brring.*

Mabel Stevens stared at the glass of gin, raised it to her lips, and drank its musty fullness in one great gulp.

In junipero veritas. . . .

Was it the liquor's bite or her angry tears that distorted the shape of the room around her, and amplified the sound of rain outside her window in St. Ebbe's?

"You stupid bugger, Art, if I told you once, I've told you a thousand times, nothing good ever comes from going to a writers' conference!"

Chapter 9

KYRIE, ELEISON

RICHARD J. FOSTER

The telephone conversation with the widow Stevens was the last call made from the Christhaven lodge. Moments later Bent tried to phone his son-in-law and found that the line was dead.

"Cut by the murderer, no doubt," speculated Hastings. "I wouldn't be surprised if he . . . or she," he continued pointedly, glancing over at Shirley, "won't have us *all* floating in that pool by tomorrow."

"Breakfast is ready," sang out Felicity.

"I'm ready too," said Johns, stumbling over a chair in his rush to respond to the sweetness of Felicity's voice.

"We really should eat," declared Gloster, trying to bring some sense of normalcy to the chaotic situation.

Lynne came to the rescue as she often did for her boss. She coaxed everyone downstairs and into the cozy dining room. The big bay windows faced Pikes Peak, and sunlight was streaming through them. *At least the storm has finally stopped,* she sighed to herself; *may it mean the end of this madness as well.* It was a half wish, a half prayer, but in either case it was in vain.

Lynne volunteered Willer to say the grace. It was one of those enthusiastic Baptist prayers that Hastings deplored. He refused to bow his head, and he refused to close his eyes. His defiance proved to be for the better, for in the midst of Willer's all-too-happy prayer, Hastings spotted something huge, something large and furry, rush past the window and disappear into the drifting snow.

"Holy crackers," shouted Hastings, "a bear!" Everyone jumped, but Hastings's bear had disappeared by the time they turned to look. "I tell you, there's a bear out there!"

"Are you sure it was a bear," queried Agatha, "and not just Whitewater Rivers in that big fur coat?"

"Whitewater's dead," insisted Adolphssohn. "I helped carry him to the balcony, and I know a dead body when I see one."

"I'm not so sure he's dead," gurgled Johns.

"It's just like a publisher to fake his own death to seek vengeance on authors, especially poets," said Agatha. "They're always out to do us in one way or another."

"It was a bear!" No matter how loud Hastings shouted, he was ignored. "I saw it with my own eyes!"

"Do you really think it was Whitewater?" puzzled Shirley. "I thought I could trust him."

"A great big furry bear," said Hastings over and over again.

"Ain't no bear that I ever seen out at this time of year." The shepherd Bent had appeared at the doorway, wet snow clinging to his moccasin-styled boots, and decided to interpolate himself immediately into the conversation. "Besides, ain't no bear done this." He held up two telephone wires that obviously had been cut. "And ain't no bear that I ever seen carry these with 'em." He tossed a pair of wire cutters on the table.

"Oh my, oh my," squealed Shirley. "You don't suppose that Whitewater—"

"Whitewater's dead!" retorted Adolphssohn.

"Then why isn't he in the pool with Yates and Stevens?" asked Willer.

"Dear me, I just don't know whether to finish my eulogy to Mr. Rivers or not," moaned Agatha. "I had such a good start on it. Iambic pentameter. Eulogies should always be in iambic pentameter, don't you think? Would you like to hear the first line?"

"Not now, dear Agatha," said Willer, leaping to the rescue, embracing her in a warm hug. "Later you can read me everything you've written, and we can discuss all your feelings about it."

"I've got a theory about poetry as the progenitor of feelings," whispered Johns to Felicity at the back table. "Later in my room I'll tell you all about it." Felicity smiled like Browning's Last Duchess.

"This isn't coffee," said Hastings, spewing black liquid all over the table in disgust. "It's decaf!"

"Where did you find those wire cutters?" asked Gloster, feigning an interest in this new detail. The shepherd stood still, his eyes studying Gloster's. Unable to stare the shepherd down, Gloster dropped his eyes to the floor. "No matter," muttered Gloster, lifting his head and attempting to return to the conversation. "The killer could have put the cutters anywhere, even in someone's luggage, just to confuse us. Besides, we really must eat. The food is getting cold. And we must not forget why we came here. . . ."

He's really not very good at impromptu speaking, mused Lynne. *He does much better when he writes it out. When he wings it, he always splits the infinitives, pitches his voice higher than normal, and gestures more than necessary.*

Why, after all, are we here? she mused further. Why did her boss invite these particular authors, and why to this particular place? She thought about the early planning stages of the meeting when he turned down a generous benefactor who offered to pay for the meeting if it would be held at the Airport Hilton in Chicago. Instead, he insisted on an isolated location, free of outside knowledge or interference.

Lynne noticed that her breathing had become more rapid, her thoughts darting to three days before when she had gone into Gloster's office, announcing that a major blizzard was predicted for the region where Christhaven was located. He merely smiled back at her, smiled and rocked back in his desk chair, smiled the smile of the Cheshire cat. It seemed strange to her then; now it seemed ominous.

"By the way," said Bent, interrupting Gloster's meandering, "where's that there lady with the beads? I have a few questions for her."

"Magdalene Smith?" Gloster was feeling in charge now. "S. J., where's Magdalene?"

"I . . . I don't know."

"What do you mean, you don't know? She's your wife," intoned Gloster, slipping into a self-righteous leadership mode. "For God's sake, man, she was the only woman who didn't sleep with the others last night. You were supposed to take care of her."

"We . . . we had a fight."

"About what?"

"Nothing an Evangelical would know about," shot Smith back in self-defense.

"It doesn't matter what you were tiffing about. All that matters really is her whereabouts this morning."

"The truth is, I've lost track of her."

"St. Christopher, preserve us," moaned Hastings, dropping his head into his hands, mourning as much the lost Magdalene as the deposed patron saint.

"You see, we had this argument. . . . She got mad, and I got mad, and she told me to leave. So what was I supposed to do, wait for an engraved invitation? I grabbed pillow, sheets, spread, and left. What else could I do? It was four in the morning. I went into the nearest room, found an empty bed, and went to sleep. I haven't seen her since then. Do you know what she called me?"

"I don't really care what she called you," retorted Gloster. "I just want to know where she is."

"'Son of an S. J.,' that's what she called me!"

"Was your bedspread yellow and apple green plaid?" asked Shirley. "And were the sheets lime?"

"How should I know? It was dark, and I couldn't see a thing."

"And what about your shoes? Are you missing a shoe?"

"Now that you mention it. . . ."

"So it was you who invaded our bedroom last night."

"How was I to know where I was going?" he asked, turning slowly toward Adolphssohn and Willer. "All I did was sleep! Just ask them."

"Shoes and sheets ain't the point right now," said Bent, stroking his whiskers. "The point is, one of you is missin', and this time it's a woman."

Willer hugged Shirley. Johns hugged Felicity. Agatha hugged her journal.

"I'm going to my, to our, room," announced Philippa. Having failed to get the reaction she desired, she turned and made a monarch's march up the staircase.

"Isn't anyone going to eat?" asked Felicity sweetly.

"I'm eating," mumbled Johns, stuffing bacon and eggs into his mouth. "I'm eating." But no one else made a move toward the table. They just stood where they were, as if waiting for something to happen. . . .

Two sharp reports broke the silence.

"Take that, you rascals . . . you murderers . . . you intruders!"

Hastings hit the floor face first. Johns stood up at the table and would have run for the front stairs if he hadn't tripped on his chair, upending his plate of food and cup of coffee on his corduroy jacket. By this time Gloster and Adolphssohn were halfway up the stairs, with Bent close behind. Willer, his first thought being the safety of the women, stayed in the dining room. Smitty got as far as the bottom of the stairs, petulantly demanding to know what had happened. "Oh, it's nothing really," said Hastings, trying to regain his balance and his composure. "It's just another beastly killing."

Inside Room 15 Adolphssohn found Philippa, a pistol in her right hand. "Thieves, robbers, murderers, take that!" Another report hit the air, and another.

"Now, now, lady, just calm down," said Bent, pushing his way past Gloster and Adolphssohn.

Panting heavily, beads of sweat rolling down her forehead, she let the pistol drop to the floor and put her slippered foot over it.

"That's a good girl," said Bent. "Now what's goin' on here?"

"It was her . . . she . . . and someone in that big fur coat. I couldn't see who was wearing the coat. They were here on that bed doing only-God-knows-what."

"Whoa, hold on there! Let's take this one thing at a time. You said her—"

"*She,*" insisted Philippa grammatically.

"Who is *her, she?* Was it this missin' woman, the one with all them beads?"

Hastings and some others from downstairs had braved the climb and were pushing now into the bedroom.

"Of course not, you fool. It was Emma, Emma Syss! She was right there on that bed. I saw her as plain as day. And she was with somebody—somebody wearing that fur coat!"

"You sure it wasn't a bear?" whelped Hastings.

"Don't be absurd, you little wimp! It must have been a man, tall and muscular, but I couldn't see his face."

"Whitewater?" gasped Shirley. She had been the one to get the publisher to finance this gathering in the first place. Deep down, she knew that once they met him, their reservations about this publisher with the unfortunate reputation would be overcome by his natural wit and wisdom. She herself had just broken long-standing contracts with two other publishing houses just to work with him . . . but now this! She felt betrayed, besmirched.

"Hold on there," said Bent. "We don't know that it was Whitewater. We don't even know if he's alive or dead. All we know is that his body was on the balcony, wrapped in that coat, and this mornin' he was gone. That's all we know. Let's not jump the gun. But speaking of guns, old lady, where did you get that there shootin' iron?"

"Agatha gave it to me after my husband died. I keep it in my handbag for protection." The two widows' eyes met. "Well, when I saw those two, I instinctively pulled it out. I was just trying to warn them not to hurt me. I tried to shoot the foot of the person wearing the coat, but accidentally shot him—or her—in the hand."

"What happened then?"

"They both ran out to the deck."

"Who did you say the woman was?"

"Emma Syss!"

"Irma Cyst?"

"Emma Syss. Rhymes with *nemesis,* without the *n.*"

"Emma Syss's first initial," volunteered Hastings, "is *N.*"

"Nemesis, schemesis, she's a writer," said Philippa in a fit of pique, "but she'll never get into the Authors' Guild, I'll tell you that right now."

"How is it, old lady, that you're the only one who has ever seen this Emma Syss around here?" asked Hastings. "Don't you think some of the rest of us should have seen her?"

"Only Li'l Harold could ask a question like that," pouted Philippa.

"I don't believe Emma Syss is here at all," continued Hastings. "In fact, I don't believe Emma Syss even exists. I understand all her books are ghostwritten."

"Who," asked Gloster, "would want to take credit for writing that kind of self-serving, head-bashing tripe?"

"Now listen here, you phony New England transplant!" shouted Philippa, puncturing the balloon of Hastings's neo-

Bostonian reserve (he had lived in the northeast for only five years) and reducing his body language to a slithery, southern Californian style.

"What do you know, you high priestess of high church idiocy?" countered Hastings. "I think you're crazy!" (Philippa was a cultured Episcopalian. A recent convert to Catholicism, Hastings viewed Episcopalians as worse than Baptists; at least Baptists were honest about their heresy, but Episcopalians . . . well, they had 'the form of godliness but denied the power thereof.')

"Are you calling me a liar, you pipsqueak?"

"You antinomian Arian heretic, you!"

"This ain't no time for your petty writers' squabbles," said Bent, stepping in between Philippa and Hastings. "I don't even know what you're arguing about and figure it wouldn't matter even if I did. We got to find us a killer, or killers, and this here Emmy Mist is as much a suspect as anyone else. In fact, I've been watching a lot of ya, and ya're all suspects in my mind."

"Emma Syss! I told you, her name is Emma Syss!"

"Emmy, Emma, it don't make no difference; she's still a suspect. Now everyone go down to the fireplace room, and let's see if we can't figure this thing out."

"Shouldn't we be going after Emma and Whitewater?" asked Philippa.

"Shouldn't we be trying to find Magdalene?" interjected Shirley.

"Shouldn't we be eating?" urged Johns.

"I'm going to look for Magdalene," announced Adolphssohn.

"I'll go with you," said Willer, stepping up to the breach for the first time. "I saw some snowshoes in the entryway. We can use them."

"You ain't goin' nowhere," said Bent. "I'm in charge here."

"You're not in charge of anybody or anything," countered Adolphssohn. "All we have is your word that your son-in-law is the sheriff and that he deputized you. Actually, we don't have any idea who you are. We've all read *Mouse Trap* and know how the so-called policeman was the murderer. So don't come to me, spouting about who's in charge. I'm going to look for Magdalene."

The Lutheran and the Baptist ministers made their way down the stairs to look for the Catholic.

Everyone's tired and cranky, thought Lynne to herself, a wave of weariness washing over her. *I don't know whom to trust anymore. The people I've known for years I'm suddenly unsure about.*

Gloster was fidgety too, transferring the ascetical earmuff first from one ear to the other and then back again. The others, though they remained in the same room, separated into smaller groups.

Adolphssohn and Willer had put on the red and black parkas and snowshoes they found in the entryway and were now well out into the snow. Neither had thought to bring dark glasses, and the glare from the sun made sight difficult.

"You check the woods down by the lake, Wesley, and I'll look around those cabins up on the hill."

"Don't you think we should stick together?"

"It would be safer, but it would also slow down the search. We have no other choice but to split up. *Necessitas absoluta.* Be strong, my friend. Remember who we are, *ecclesia militans.*"

"*Ecclesia triumphans!*" warbled Willer, trying to sound a positive note.

After he had gone about a football field's length up the hill, Adolphssohn stopped to rest. Looking back he could see Willer's tracks leading down toward the trees; all signs of Willer himself had disappeared. He turned and climbed upward toward the cabins, heart pounding, lungs heaving in the thin mountain air. His goal was to find Magdalene, of course, but his mind was not intent on that alone.

Somehow, in spite of the desperateness of the situation, Adolphssohn found himself rehearsing a long-forgotten theological debate from his seminary days. "*Was it* posse peccare

. . . non posse peccare . . . non posse non peccare. *We are able to sin . . . we are not able to sin . . . we are not able not to sin."*

Which is it? he mused. *I think the third option,* non posse non peccare . . . *we are not able not to sin.* Smiling, he remembered the comment of a crusty old professor, "I like you, Adolphssohn—your Lutheranism has a touch of Calvin in it!"

He did not have much time to bask in his newly found theological conviction. Just then he saw a movement at the farthest cabin. He dropped to the snow, now keenly aware that the red and black plaid of his parka stood out like a huge checkerboard on a white cloth. Dies ater! *I wish I'd been more careful! If anyone's up there, they'll know I'm coming.*

After a moment he raised his head slowly, straining to see further. Nothing. But just when he began to sit up, he saw a large figure run swiftly across the snow and disappear into the highest cabin.

That may be the man in the fur coat, he thought, *or it may not.* He lay still, his body heat melting the snow under him, the cold water freezing his shirt collar. After a half hour, his curiosity began to conquer his fear. He gallumphed as quickly and discreetly as the snowshoes allowed, reaching the first cabin at last. Dodging behind it, he used the second cabin as a cover to approach the third, making his way toward the topmost cabin. There, he slipped off the snowshoes and crept around to the side window. Cautiously he peered inside. At first he saw nothing. Then his eyes focused on a single chair in the middle of the room. He could see that someone was seated in the chair, but he couldn't tell who it was because the person faced the other way. He could see also that the person was wearing the big fur coat.

He noticed something else. Whoever was wearing the fur coat was not in charge of things because he—or she—was bound hand and foot to the chair.

Gagged too, he noticed, for he could now make out a black handkerchief around the back of his—her—head.

Adolphssohn crept around to the front of the cabin to get a better view from those windows, but they were covered with plywood. "I've got to get inside," he muttered to himself. "It could be Magdalene in that chair." He laid both hands on the wooden door and, giving a tremendous shove, broke in, shouting at the same time *"Veni, vidi, vici!"* Once inside, he came face to face with the person in the chair, whose eyes were trying to warn him of the danger. Too late. A hard wooden ax handle crashed against his skull.

Trying to fight the blackness that began to envelope him, he crumpled to the floor. Blood gushed from his wound, blinding him in the left eye. He strained to see his assailant. He thought he saw the form lunge toward him. Instinctively he rolled over three times, thus saving himself from a fatal knife thrust. As the attacker prepared to lunge again, vision returned to Adolphssohn's right eye.

"Emma Syss!"

She was on him with a fury. Her blade sank into his arm. He dug the heel of his boot into her midriff and flung her backward, the knife flying from her hand. Then, in spite of the pain, he lunged at her. Over and over they rolled, knocking over the chair and the person on it. He was amazed at Emma's strength. True, she was a big woman, but he had fought big men before in his college wrestling days, and she matched any of them.

Nobody seemed to be winning as they caromed about the floor for what seemed like hours. He was weakening from his wounds, and his mind slipped backward to the time when he had actually met her. It was at the Christian Booksellers Convention the year they met in New Orleans. She had been proper but curt, making a caustic comment about his pipe and about how pipe smokers were going to burn in the fires of Hell. She wouldn't believe he didn't smoke or carried the pipe only as a prop. *"Non posse non peccare,"* he remembered having said, but he remembered something else. The cane. Emma Syss walked with a cane!

During this lapse of concentration, the assailant had managed to slip from his grasp, retrieve the knife, and begin the assault anew. Adolphssohn grabbed the knife arm with his left hand and with his right, reached up. He grabbed the assailant's hair and with one movement ripped off what must have been a rubber face mask.

"Et tu, Brute?" he gasped, the strength slipping from his arms, allowing the assailant's knife to sink swiftly into his heart. As blackness closed in around him, he heard the figure standing over him chanting softly, *"Kyrie, eleison . . . Christe, eleison . . . Kyrie, eleison."*

Chapter 10

"AVENGE, O LORD, THY SLAUGHTERED SAINTS"

EMILIE GRIFFIN

Halfway down the snowy slope, Willer began to get an uneasy feeling. It was a sudden stab of guilt, a knot of fear in his vitals. A premonition—yes, that's what it was.

He knew he was heading the wrong way. First of all, there was nothing ahead of him, nothing but a white expanse, trackless, without clues or leads, no paths or possibilities to pursue. But more than observation told him he was headed wrong. Reason also said he was off course. And then there was this baffling inner voice, intuition, commanding him, *Turn back, turn back!* No chance of finding the Lady Magdalene, or the murderer, by descending the snowy hill. . . .

As so often when under pressure, he moved into high poetic mode. Poetry long buried in his consciousness fought its way up to the surface, welled up to the top of his mind. *No, that way madness lies!* Willer thought, then knew right away that it was *King Lear.*

From the looks of it, Dolph had guessed right once again in that maddening way he had. With bull's-eye marksmanship, Dolph had chosen the better path, taken the high road while he, Wes, had taken the low. "I'll be in Scotland afore ye. . . ."

Willer felt inferior and foolish as he often did when competing with Dolph. That blamed Lutheran, always sticking his theses on some dumb door, then saying he could do no other! He got away with things that Willer could never pull off. At the same time, Willer loved both the rivalry and the rival. If something happened to Dolph. . . .

What if Dolph, by guessing right, had already stumbled into the killer's path? Alone? How foolish they had been to part company! he realized. One at a time they were no match for . . . the bear, the baffling murderer, the nemesis.

Willer turned, surveyed the steep ascent, and began to puff his way up the powdery slope. It was bitterly cold. Sunlight blazed across the white, unrelenting expanse. His ankles felt the pain of the clumsy snowshoes.

On his way up, he kept trying to puzzle out a motive. Who would want to seize Magdalene? What reason could anyone have for trying to put her away?

Another puzzlement. Why were he and Dolph more concerned about it than Smitty? Was this blissful marriage of theirs as blessed as it appeared?

And didn't Smitty's accidental night with the ladies suggest a wandering eye? A wandering foot, at the very least? Oh, what he, Wes, wouldn't give for a night like Smitty's in the hencoop, even if nothing in particular actually took place. Oh, the fantasy, the proximity, the nearness of it all! The hairpins and the curling irons, the fragrance and the cold cream!

When he arrived at that point on the hill where he and Adolphssohn had parted, he still had no good theories. He looked back at Christhaven for a moment. . . .

Suddenly an odd thought struck him. As long as he couldn't see any of the others, how could he be sure any of them were still alive? Even his own existence seemed to be shaky. What if a massacre was going on, a serial murder? What if all of them were to be slaughtered by this cruel murderer or murderers? Cold as he was, Willer felt a new kind of chill, an inner chill of desperation. Then these words flooded his mind:

Avenge, O Lord, your slaughtered saints. . . .

Was it Shakespeare? Milton? Iambic pentameter for sure. From a sonnet possibly. What flash of intuition, what angelic messenger put it in his mind just then? Whatever, whoever, he was needed. Dolph needed him. Maybe even Magdalene. They were in danger. Leaving the contemplative mode, he took great cowboy strides upslope.

Soon he sighted the mountain cabin, distant but clear in the thin mountain air. Outside, everything was peaceful and still. But what about those little windows? What was going on behind them? Was it his imagination? Didn't he see . . . something . . . shapes moving, lunging across the window openings, making crazy images on the panes?

Of course! There was a struggle going on inside, something like a fistfight or a wrestling match. Instinctively he took refuge behind a tree trunk. He had no weapon, no way to attack or defend.

But Dolph might need his help. He had to rush the cabin. Now he heard shouts, even screams, like an animal cry. Then a sudden loud noise. Was that a door bursting open on the far side of the cabin? No sense holding back—he had to rush in.

Sure enough, as he pulled the door open, the first thing he saw was the far door open, banging back and forth as though someone had just fled.

And bodies on the floor, not one but two. Instead of going to the bodies first, he tore across the room, looking out of the wildly swinging door. But there was no one in sight. Wherever the murderer had gone to, he or she was not behind the door but had vanished, it seemed, into a wilderness of snow.

Completely baffled now, Willer returned to survey the bodies lying on the floor. Was that hideous woman Emma Syss actually dead? Why was she wearing Dolph's red and black jacket, just like the one he himself had on? She seemed even taller than he remembered and had a huge gash in her chest. And was that Magdalene lying next to her, deader than a doornail?

Should he disturb the bodies? Wasn't that Bent the shepherd's role? But was that goofy pseudodetective capable of investigating anything? And where was Dolph, why wasn't he here, if he had been the first one up the hill?

The sight of Magdalene was heartbreaking at first. Could anyone look so holy in death? She was Snow White under glass. How like her to die with her hands piously folded, plaiting her rosary beads, in an attitude of prayer. Or was that the murderer's ironic finale before he or she fled?

The popery thickens, Willer thought. Obviously there was a message built into this wilderness massacre—he just wished he knew what it was.

He knelt down beside the bodies, trying to decide whether or not to tamper with the evidence. Such an odd frame for a dame, he thought, looking at Emma's huge body at rest. And then he realized—it was not a face but a face mask. Hastily pulled over the head of the corpse, the wrinkling rubber was a dead giveaway. He pulled the mask away and found the real face underneath.

Oh my God! Dolph Adolphssohn!! Christ have mercy!!!

And to make matters worse, there was a pamphlet clutched in his hand.

NULLA SALUS EXTRA ECCLESIAM
A Publication of
The Catholic Truth Society

It was one of those terrible tracts that Catholics used to circulate, proving they were the only ones with a corner on salvation.

"Those sniveling, squealing Sons of the Inquisition!" shouted Willer, his indignation coming quickly to a boil. *Those bloody Catholics are still sinister folk, no matter how they turn up in sheep's clothing! No use trying to trust people who are so wrongheaded. It just goes to show you what comes of being kind to your enemies.*

Even as he said it, he felt a twinge of guilt. For there, next to his beloved Dolph, was Magdalene, prayerfully and papistically dead. His feelings overwhelmed him now. He found himself filling up with rage. The more fool he for having looked up to her as a prayer mentor, for having read her holy books on the sly, hiding them inside the *New Baptist Hymnal* so he wouldn't be found out during Wednesday night service!

Now he felt really betrayed. To think that Magdalene was dead because she had killed Dolph. Or was it the other way around? Had Dolph threatened Magdalene, and she had assaulted him in return? How could this frail creature have assaulted anyone? Or was she just the occasion for his death, not its cause?

Willer was overcome with rage, confusion, and grief. The tears began to flow; he was hurting way deep down.

> Avenge, O Lord, thy slaughtered saints, whose bones
> Lie scattered on the Alpine mountains cold,
> Even them who kept thy truth so pure of old
> When all our Fathers worshipped stocks and stones
> Forget not: in thy book record their groans. . . .

Unbelievable! It was Milton, and he was quoting it exactly from memory! How many years since he had memorized those words, pacing up and down before Friday afternoon recitation class! Now, it seemed, nothing but grandiose, ennobled measures could match the high level of his woe.

> Who were thy Sheep and in their ancient Fold
> Slain by the bloody Piedmontese that rolled
> Mother with Infant down the rocks.

That was it! They were murdered because they were Protestants! It was a poem about the wicked Papists. . . .

> . . . their moans
> The Vales redoubled to the Hills, and they
> To Heaven. Their martyred blood and ashes sow. . .
> O'er all the Italian fields where still doth sway
> The triple Tyrant: that from these may grow
> A hundredfold, who having learnt thy way
> Early may fly the Babylonian woe.

I can't believe it, he thought. *I can't believe that Dolph is dead, that Magdalene is also dead. I can't believe that I recited a sonnet of Milton's all the way through without a mistake. . . .*

But the Lord must be telling me something here. The "triple tyrant," why that's the pope all right. . . and the "Babylonian woe," that's popery, that's Magdalene and Smitty for a start. Here I was, mourning that female, when she was probably, like Helen of Troy, the cause of it all!

With something less than gallantry, Willer poked a cowboy boot into the body of the angelic Magdalene.

"Don't look so innocent, you wench! You led my holy Lutheran pal down the proverbial garden path. You enchanted him with your R. C. sorcery! You inveigled him to his death—then clamped the face of Emma Syss over his sweet face to disguise your brutal deed!"

"I'm not dead, Wes; I'm just having an OOBE," came an eerie voice that startled Willer out of his rage and grief, "an out-of-body experience."

"Who are you?"

"It's me, Magdalene."

"But where are you?"

"I'm slowly phasing back into my body after the most incredible experience."

Willer looked around frantically. Magdalene's body was as still as a corpse. In fact, to all intents and purposes she was dead. When he pinched her cheek, it felt cold. But then, of course, the cabin was cold, and no doubt his face felt just as chilly right now.

"Wes, it's me. . . ."

Where was her voice coming from?

"I'm looking down on you and Dolph."

Her face was without animation, and her lips had not moved.

"I'm up here around the ceiling, but you can't see me. I never believed a word about near-death experiences, Raymond Moody and all that," Magdalene continued cheerily, "but now I know it's for real. Hmmmph!" It was a sort of muffled giggle.

"Is this some more of your Catholic hocus-pocus? Declare yourself, or I'll have you reported to the Society for Psychical Research!"

"Oh, really, is there a Colorado chapter?"

Now he saw her stir—her lips began to twitch ever so slightly.

"So you are alive, you really are. Now wait. If you're alive, is there a chance we could also revive Dolph?"

"I think Dolph must have definitely passed over. He's in a different category altogether."

"You're sure of that?"

"Well, as sure as I can get. If you could just have seen the angels, leading him into paradise. . . . Oh Wes, I was so moved."

"It's really like that? Were you in a trance, or what? Oh well, you can tell me the details later. Right now, what about the murder? Can you remember?"

Magdalene was alive, after all. Slowly she stirred, making efforts to sit up, but she seemed completely drained of strength.

"They struggled here. Emma Syss hit him over the head with an ax. I tried to warn him, but I was tied in that chair, wearing the big bear coat. . . ."

Willer found himself feeling skeptical, wanting to believe her but hardly daring to. Had she seen the fight, the struggle? What had become of the real murderer, and if it wasn't Emma Syss, who was it? Unfortunately, Magdalene had seen nothing, for the fighting all took place behind her back, and once Emma Syss had removed the rubber mask, his or her identity remained hidden.

"But after the murder I'm sure I heard the killer say, '*Kyrie, eleison; Christe, eleison; Kyrie, eleison,*' meaning 'Lord, have mercy, Christ, have mercy, Lord, have mercy.'"

"What about the voice? Did you recognize it?"

"Not really. It could have been a woman's voice, but more likely a man's. It was very deep."

Well, at least the foe was a Christian, Willer thought. *Or was he really a persecutor of Christians? Wasn't he using parts of the eucharistic service to cast suspicion on the Catholics gathered ecumenically with their Protestant counterparts at Christhaven? Was he an agent of the triple tyrant? Or trying to set Christian ecumenism back three hundred years?*

"We've established one thing. Whoever the murderer is, it should be easy to spot him. Wearing that big old bear coat. It's not so easy to hide when you're all wrapped up in something like that."

Magdalene looked around. Sure enough, the big shaggy coat was nowhere to be seen. "He or she must have conked me over the head, then took the coat and made tracks." She was sitting up now, rubbing the top of her head thoughtfully, but she looked woozy.

"We've got to get back to the lodge—they'll be wondering about us," Willer said. "Can you walk, Maggie? Are you well enough?"

After several attempts to head down the snowy hill, Magdalene collapsed, rosary beads in hand. Willer saw no solution but to carry her. He scooped her slender person up into his arms, feeling rather like Rhett Butler taking Scarlett O'Hara up the plantation staircase. *She might be a Papist,* he mused, *but she did have a pleasant way of snuggling in. . . .*

Would Smitty be jealous? he asked himself as he stumbled down the slope. *Wasn't Smitty the prime suspect, after all? Who else would utter the words* Kyrie, eleison, Christe, eleison, Kyrie, eleison *after polishing someone off? His behavior had been suspect from the start. Anyone trained by the Jesuits and with the initials S. J. was definitely under a cloud.*

At the door to the lodge, Willer shouldered the door open and stashed the weakened Magdalene on the sofa nearest the entrance, disturbing a whoopee cushion that burbled the melody of "Nearer, My God, to Thee."

Lord help us, where was everybody? The lodge seemed abandoned. But still, Willer felt a sinister presence, as though the murderer might be waiting behind any door.

Pausing only for a brief moment of prayer, Willer barged into the main room of the lodge. It was empty, but the fire was blazing.

In the room where the organ was, he got his first ugly surprise. Stretched out on the floor in a dead faint were Shirley, Felicity, Agatha, and Johns.

In a near panic, Willer headed for the staircase. Bounding to the top, he saw what he was most afraid of. Philippa and Gloster flat on the floor. Had they fainted, or were they dead? Willer wouldn't even dare to suppose it. They had been sprinkled by sleep dust, they had been stunned by gamma rays . . . anything but death in such numbers.

But where were the others? Smitty? Hastings? Bent?

In a terror, he rushed down to the swimming pool. That would be the place to find the missing bodies. But when he got there, the rude shock became even ruder. The swimming pool was empty. Even the bodies of Yates and Stevens had disappeared.

Christhaven was a ghost town, full of empty spaces where the dead bodies used to be; and where the live bodies used to be, a bunch of other people who looked as though they might sleep a thousand years.

The powerful odor of chlorine cleared his head. It was like getting a high, an inspiration. Suddenly the whole scenario, the who-did-what-to-whom-and-why leapt into his mind, and he was sure he could put the pieces together now or later in a court of law.

He headed back through the lodge, planning to take Magdalene with him to the van and away from this dreadful place before it was too late.

"Going somewhere, Reverend Willer?" It was definitely the voice of the Wicked Witch of the West. "You'll spoil the fun. Our little party's just beginning."

He turned to see a figure in a World War I gas mask, looking like a Martian in a novel by H. G. Wells. Whoever it was, the image began to shimmer and melt as Willer fainted dead away.

Chapter 11

THE MUSE IS MUCH AMUSED

LUCI SHAW

It was three in the afternoon. As soon as Willer hit the floor by the organ, overcome by the gas, one of the bodies began to stir.

It was Agatha, whose movements, at first jerky and random, soon became purposeful. Slowly she rose to her knees, then stood, swaying a little, careful not to touch or disturb the others, who were still dead to the world.

Did I actually think "dead to the world?" she asked herself, beginning to giggle inwardly. She had cultivated the reputation as an emotional yo-yo to the point where she *was* an emotional yo-yo. And though she gave the impression of being a mixed bag—a poet whose sensibilities canceled out her sense, a writer shielded from the real world in a chrysalis of rhyme, rhythm, and abstraction—she was, from time to time, actually capable of rational thought. Underneath her flighty esthetic carapace and in spite of her excursions into mystical spirituality, she cherished the instincts of a hard-boiled businesswoman with a nose for the hard sell, the big break. She knew this would have come as a surprise to most of those gathered at Christhaven (it often surprised Agatha herself) with one exception. And, thank Heaven, he wasn't talking.

Still slightly dizzy, Agatha wondered if she were hallucinating. Weird thumps and scratches and pinging sounds emanated from around the corner where the pay phone was housed. Could someone be fixing the phone line? But who? Everyone capable of such an arcane task was dead, fled, or unconscious.

Her mind was drifting back to the comatose corpses still slumbering as if their lives depended on it (perhaps they did) when suddenly she choked. *My journal! Where did I leave my journal?* One of Agatha's worst nightmares was that she might lose this always-ready receptacle for her ongoing stream of consciousness, and such a loss would be double damning now, for within its rigorously guarded pages were not only her elegies but also her running commentary, in the form of a checklist, cataloging every detail of the events of this climactic week. If the journal were to fall into the wrong hands, all would be lost.

Gingerly, the silver-haired poet poked around the knees and elbows among the pile of recumbent writers. Ahhh, at last she felt the cloth bound corner of the incriminating volume poking out from under the body of Johns, who was sonorously snoring, and she retrieved it with a sigh of relief. He hadn't moved. It was a shame he'd have to go. A *fine* poet in spite of his moral turpitude. But death might even enhance his literary reputation.

She felt a slight nausea. She was sure it would be nothing like what the others would feel when they awoke, disoriented, even deranged. They'd be *non compos mentis* and *sub rosa* for a couple of days, as would Philippa and Gloster upstairs (she could use Latin tags just as easily as Dolph had). And then, the nerve gas would complete its deadly work, rendering them permanently unable to think, write, or speak. Now *that* was true nemesis.

Amazing how quickly her accomplice's chemical had acted! But it was her idea to fall insensible along with the rest, after inhaling a far milder preparation. Suspicion would surely be directed away from her now.

Moving to the window and flipping open her journal for reference, she began to count on her fingers (computation had never been her forte). . . .

Dead: Yates, Adolphssohn, Stevens. *Ironic. Now Nate and Dolph could conduct their postcolloquial confab in some celestial sphere. Long-winded as they were, their conversation now could go on eternally.*

Soon to be permanently incapacitated: Felicity, Shirley, Johns, Gloster, Magdalene, Willer, Lynne, and Philippa. *Too bad Philippa hadn't taken her hint and used the pistol—"Such a sensitive gift, Agatha!"—on herself. It would have been a quicker and easier way to go.*

Still remaining to be dealt with: Hastings, Smitty, and Rivers. . . .

Rivers? His unaccountable disappearance and the circumstances of his resuscitation were mysterious enough to perplex the others and also that crooked shepherd Bent.

Rivers and she herself—how ironic that the two of them, the lone publishers in the group, had ended up as coconspirators. . . .

It had all begun years before, she recalled, when Yates, with *It Hurts When It Hurts,* had so subtly undercut her own publishing house's forthcoming book *The Popularity of Pain;* she had had to withdraw it before publication for fear of being sued for plagiarism. Yates had been making headlines by throwing himself out of open windows to experience firsthand how much it hurt. His primary research had been impressive, she had to admit.

And then Gloster had played the same game; he had got there first. If it hadn't been for the one-upmanship of George, that serpent of spirituality, Rivers's proposed publication of *Money, Sex, and Pain,* a treatise on Christian sadomasochism, would have been a runaway bestseller. As everyone in publishing knows, controversy breeds super-sales, and Rivers couldn't have resisted the temptation. But few Evangelical publishing houses would have dared the topic.

That had been hers and Rivers's double strength—to find the unexplored niches in the Christian Booksellers Association market, and to fill them with "mind- and soul-stretching books."

Until Yates and Gloster. . . .

Ahhh, Gloster—was he with her and Rivers now, or was he against them? Gloster's motives and his personality had remained dark enigmas to her, his facile heartiness clearly a cover-up for the inner motives at work within him.

After all, it was he who had arranged for this isolated gathering, this remote resort. And, like other spiritual celebrities in the news these days, he might even have precipitated the bad weather by that old technique—faith forecasting. Even Lynne, his loyal assistant, had suspected something. Perhaps simplicity wasn't all that it was trumped up to be. Perhaps complicity would better describe him

Gloster's ever-present, flashily ascetic earmuff suddenly leaped into significance in her searching mind. (Usually she didn't have a clue. But her detective instincts were being quickly and sharply honed.) Did the muff conceal some electronic device—some miniature radio transceiver with which he could communicate with . . . God knew whom? No possibility should be discounted.

Authors. . . .

Not just Gloster but the whole damned, conniving pack of them.

Where was their humility?

Where were their rings of endless light, their own celebration of discipline, their freedom of simplicity, when it came to escalating royalties and foreign rights?

How could they trumpet Christian virtues in their books and then sell their souls, like marketable commodities, to the highest bidder, competing shamelessly for the biggest advances, the juiciest promotional campaigns, appearances on the "Geraldo" show, their book titles imprinted on book bags at CBA?

Well, they've brought all this down on their own heads!

Through the western window Agatha looked out on the snowy landscape, every fence post and tree and fieldstone coated with billowing curves of white purity, the far peaks of the Rockies fiercely hallowed by the golden gleams of the setting sun. But underneath? The decay, the rotting wood, the slime of dead leaves, the sleeping maggots. . . .

It was an existential metaphor. Quickly she scribbled it in her journal—in the section reserved for reflecting on her own reflections (a literary form she had elevated to a fine art). It was all to be embodied in *God in the Doghouse*, her metaphysical treatment of total depravity. That would set the CBA market on its ear!

She laughed gleefully, but to another hearer the sound would have seemed menacing.

The ensuing silence was broken by the shrill tone of the telephone, ringing again and again. But weren't the lines dead? Aha, that must have been where that mad shepherd-sheriff had been running: Hell-bent over the hill to the next resort to summon help from the local telephone company, Colorado Call. It must have been the repairman who had made these scraping and beeping noises.

Finally awakened out of her bemused state by the unanswered phone, she rushed across the room, around the corner to the phone booth, and seized the old-fashioned receiver from its cradle.

"Gaines Godly Publishing House—For Books You Wouldn't *Believe*," she answered, without thinking. "How may we help you?"

"Mm. Philippa d'Esprit, please. Long distance calling."

"May I say who's calling? Besides Long Distance?"

"It's her agent. I've had a lot of trouble getting through."

"Well, we've been having the most awful blizzard," explained Agatha innocently. "Can I take a message? Mm. d'Esprit can't come to the phone right now. She's somewhat indisposed. But this is one of her publishers, Agatha Gaines. Remember me? You can trust me to get the message to her."

"Well, it's about the Authors' Guild. They called last week to say they'd just elected her president *in perpetuo* because she did such a bang-up job this past year. Give her our congratulations. By the way, I noticed a detestable picture of her in last Sunday's *New York Times* book review section. She looked so strange in that huge fur coat of hers—just like a Russian bear. Please get her to send me some more appealing promotional photos, something that would enhance her image—you know, bizarre but magnificent?"

Agatha managed to suppress a gasp before she hung up. The agent's reference to Philippa's looking bearlike in a fur coat—the image was superimposed in her mind over the figure in the bear coat slipping in and out of the lodge. No one claimed to have actually seen it but Philippa. Had it really been her hallucination all along? Or was it rather not a hallucination at all but some weird mental projection of Philippa herself? Grief did strange things to highly strung artists. . . .

And then Agatha gasped again. The name Emma Syss—maybe it wasn't just "nemesis without the N." *Emesis* was the physical act of vomiting. Was Philippa, in some strange purgative aberration, trying to rid herself of the image of her detractors? Were she and Emma Syss one and the same, two inimical personalities within one ample body, both implicated in murder and mayhem?

It all seemed very farfetched, but so did everything else that had happened in the past few days. Agatha's and Philippa's common criminality—in a way it made a kind of satiric sense. The two had tracked together before, as author and publisher of *A Bone for a Pillow,* the second volume of Philippa's Generic Trilogy. Both of them were Episcopalians, widows, and had birthdays on the twenty-ninth. Both wrote violent and inscrutable poetry. And in the long and boring intervals between the murders at Christhaven, when serious literary discussion was clearly impossible, both had resorted to the game room below and competed fiercely at the Ping-Pong table.

Never look back, Agatha had reminded herself with determination. *No sense crying over spilled blood.* Swiftly she mounted the stairs. On the upstairs landing she found the unconscious Philippa and sitting next to her, looking spaced out, was Gloster. He blinked up at her.

"It's all true," he choked. "The New Age. I just dreamed I was levitating on an Astro-Jet all the way back to Wichita. I was channeling too, to an earlier incarnation—St. Thomas Aquinas (he looked complacent!). And I think my next book will be titled *Harmonic Convergence: Myth or Miracle?* Get Lynne Teal. Tell her I'm ready to dictate."

It's working, mused Agatha, amused. *He attacked New Age thinking in* Evangelism Today *last year. Now this. A total reversal. The nerve gas has attacked his ganglia. He'll be useless at the next CBA. They'll picket his publisher and burn his books.*

Suddenly Gloster's proximity to Philippa gained new significance in Agatha's mind. Had the two meditators been about to join forces? The relationships within the group had been getting stickier and were now positively mucilaginous. Who could follow the couplings, the permutations of plot, the combinations of conspiracy?

Hastings! The name sprang to her mind as if by inspiration. He was still at large. He'd told her how much he'd always envied Gloster's power and his prose style. Her mind leaped to this new possibility. She'd update him on Gloster's condition.

With old George disqualified, disenfranchised, she thought, stigmatized as a seducer of Christianity, hounded by Rave Blunt and his cohorts, Hastings would have a free hand to take over the Hilton Center for Christian Writers. All he needed was money. But soon money would be no problem.

Together with Rivers they'd build the religious empire envisioned by Gloster.

Agatha had intended to make a killing. . . .

After all, she was the author of *Listen to the Gold*. . . .

And her name wasn't Agatha Gaines for nothing!

Chapter 12

MYSTERIOUS WAYS

HAROLD FICKETT

On a spur of the private road that led to the Christhaven lodge, a mile or so back into the hills, Hastings had found a promontory, an encampment of buff-colored rocks among the aspen and pine. He sat with his legs dangling over the edge of a snow-covered boulder and looked out toward Pikes Peak. He could not see the summit. After a bright afternoon, the clouds had come back. The ceiling was still high enough that he could see the snowfields above the tree line. The second day of this murderous conference was nearly at an end. The snow on the mountains was white like the white water of waves, phosphorescent—lunar just before nightfall. The evergreens added only the darkest olive to what was otherwise a monochrome study. The undulating folds of the mountains seemed an ever-scrolling parchment, with the trees printing out the text's meaning in a language too ancient to be translated.

Hastings took a long drag on his tenth cigarette, pulling the smoke down into his lungs as if storing goods deep in a hold. He had been driven away from the authors' gathering by his nicotine addiction and also by cravings of the spirit that were less easily satisfied.

After communing with his own thoughts for well over two hours, his cheeks felt dead and rubbery and the fiery cold of his icy perch had welded his spine, seemingly, to the rock underneath him. Still he remained. He had come out from the lodge to escape its tensions, but, if anything, his own sense of uneasiness had increased. He looked once more across the steep wedge of valley at his feet to the mountains opposite him. With the summit blind to view, he could not find the focal point he wanted. Without a focus he could not place the scene within a frame. He was trying desperately to locate himself, in this scene, in his life. His own distance from the mountains wavered with his every attempt at perspective.

Feeling dizzy, trying to relax, he snapped his head to the left, popping an upper vertebra. He put out his cigarette on the rock and flipped it away. His neck was stiff; his breathing, shallow. He looked back across the valley once more. Now, the mountains themselves seemed to be moving, trundling past like elephants. He thought he felt the first tremors of an earthquake . . . and then he had to catch himself, his own vertigo casting him into free-fall. He scrambled back from the edge of the rock, closed his eyes, and took several deep breaths, inhaling slowly. He put his hands out to either side to steady himself. The moment passed—he landed where he had been, feeling the earth bearing his weight once more.

As Hastings had once confessed to Stevens, nature gave him the willies. More precisely, it sometimes brought on panic attacks, episodes of acute terror. He would have been more disturbed as he sat there, recollecting his sanity, if he had not lived with this condition long enough to understand what precipitated the attacks and why he was subjected to them. If his soul sometimes shuddered, quaked, and then flew out to meet the nothingness surrounding him, it did so only after detonations in his life that exploded his frame of reference, that shattered the context in which he hoped to live. His panic attacks were the outward and phenomenal sign of an inward and noumenal malaise.

Yates's death had been to Hastings a Big Bang that sent the once compact matter of his own mental universe accelerating away. Although no one else at Christhaven seemed to realize this, Hastings had been extremely close to Yates, had even been best friends when Hastings taught at St. Lewis College and Yates worked as an editor at *Evangelism Today* magazine. Hastings's college and Yates's magazine were two of the signal institutions in a cluster of organizations west of Chicago known, to those who worked in them, as the "Evangelical Vatican." When they met they understood at once how their personalities complemented one another: Hastings was shrewd about prose; Yates, about everything else. Hastings was one of the few people to whom the self-protective Yates opened up, and Yates was one of the few people who could stand being around someone as wide open as Hastings. A Jack Sprat couple, they licked their platters clean. Now Yates's death was certainly triggering his phobic meltdown.

Hastings had arrived at Christhaven at what he might himself term, carrying over the metaphor, critical mass. His Christian publisher had in the last two months rejected his latest novel, excoriating it as "too truthful." Hastings, in the book's defense, paraphrased Picasso: fiction is a lie that tells the truth. In the CBA market, his publisher had countered, fiction must be a lie that keeps on lying.

The text of his own life had become, as a deconstructionist would say, radically indeterminate. He felt sometimes that he was a fictional character invented by twelve different authors, each with his own idea about the plot. He had tried to make the text of his life something out of Flaubert, a natural and inevitable progression, with a marzipan surface. With Yates dead now, his own career in ruins, he found himself in a murder mystery, a genre he deplored.

Yet, weren't there fascinating correspondences between that genre and the Christian story itself? Beneath the surface of ordinary life, with its excuses and rationalizations, wasn't there raging a battle between the powers of darkness and those of light? And didn't it take a supreme detective, a fiction writer of considerable powers, to see through the surface illusion to the reality that lurked beneath? And wasn't the knowledge that enabled him to do this a product both of special revelation and the spiritual discipline the detective always displayed in searching out the truth? Wasn't the detective, in sum, another guise for the true knight of faith? Certainly many writers whose prose Hastings found execrable had launched their Father Browns with just these ideas in mind. Wasn't life itself, conceived in Christian terms, a mystery?

Suddenly Hastings spied Agatha Gaines walking along the drive below him. He waved and shouted in greeting, more than willing to abandon his reveries and drink in the milk of Agatha's kindness. Abandoning his rocky perch, he half-ran down the trail, slipping and sliding through the snow.

Her eyes were bright with excitement. She took his arm and directed their steps back toward the lodge. In fact, their arms manacled together, she drove him back through the powdery snow like the master of a dogsled competing in Alaska's Iditarod. "I have something to show you," she said.

She took him not to the lodge but to the uppermost cabin. They entered the cabin, now murky with the gathering dark outside. As he stepped across the threshold after her, Hastings saw four figures seated at a card table. Perhaps she had invited him to a select meeting to discuss the murders. He closed the door behind him and snapped on the light.

"Whitewater!" she screamed.

Whitewater, Yates, Stevens, and a very dead Adolphssohn proved to be the figures meeting in this most deathly of committees. The four corpses slumped in their chairs like card players awaiting a bid that would never be made.

Hastings wondered why Agatha had exclaimed over Rivers—who had been missing for some time—rather than Adolphssohn, whose death came as a surprise. He looked back to the publisher's corpse.

Whitewater's murder—or as it appeared now, reexecution—must have been committed in a strangely ritualistic fashion. He wore the bear coat. His lips were fastened, jabbed through, with a TRY GOD pin, around which a clown's lips had been painted in the same shade of lipstick that had crossed out the first word of PERHAPS TODAY. His lower arms and hands were folded around what proved to be three record albums, one by Dino, one by Amy Grant, and one by Sandi Patti. (Whitewater's company, CURD, Incorporated, besides publishing books, Hastings remembered, also produced records, the very ones Whitewater held among them.) His dark hair, every strand of it cut to one inch in length, had been topped with what looked at first like an old bathing cap. This turned out to be the Emma Syss mask. It seemed clear that whoever had done this to Whitewater had it in for CURD. Was the killer saying that TRY GOD was the corporation's motto, in the sense that all their profit making had to do with trying the Almighty's patience? Hastings could not agree with the killer's methods, but as a critic the killer had a point.

Agatha began to choke. Her hand to her mouth, she rushed past Hastings outside. Evidently she was as surprised by the grisly sight as he. He waited for the expected retch and splash before going out to comfort her.

He found her on her knees, scooping up handfuls of snow and pressing them to her mouth and cheeks. She looked wan and suddenly exhausted, and yet, at the same time, alive in a new way, glistening and pure, as if she were a milky white creature that had just emerged from her cocoon. She had thrown off her long fur coat, it had landed behind her in a crouching position, the shell, perhaps, of her former self.

Once she was feeling better, he took her handkerchief and wiped the last flecks of foam from her mouth and then encouraged her to come back with him to the lodge. But she insisted on going back into the cabin once more. She reached for her coat, and, before putting it back on, turned it inside out. A reversible garment, the coat could be worn with either its blueish or its taupe half out. He remembered that she had worn the red half of the shell on the outside previously, but now she chose to present the milder shade.

Back inside the cabin, she pulled out a hand-sized cloth-covered volume from one of the coat's big side pockets: her journal. She opened it up, found the place she wanted, and handed it to him. "I thought we knew what we were doing," she said.

Hastings leaned against the wall and read while Agatha paced. He had the eerie sensation that Yates had turned his frozen attention from the corpses' card game and was now looking at him disapprovingly. Yates, had he been alive, would have understood that the protagonist happening on a journal or a letter in the course of a narrative is one of the oldest and most haggard devices in fiction for conveying information. Hastings wanted to protest that he was only a character in this drama. *So lay off, bud,* he wanted to say. *Lay off, late lamented friend.*

10/16 Received a call today from Whitewater Rivers of CURD, Incorporated, who informs me that our writing group's idyll in the Coloradan cascades means no good for Christian publishing. What has been planned is nothing less than a coup d'etat, an apocalypse now, for every Christian publisher, our own Gaines Godly included. This yo-yo is going to put on her yarmulke and do some thinking.

George Gloster has selected some of the most well-known and at the same time woolly minded writers in the business. Gloster plans for all of us at Christhaven to collaborate on a book: *They Call It a Ministry.* Each participant is to contribute one chapter. Making use of the group's collective experience as writers, *They Call It a Ministry* is meant to point an all-too-accusatory finger at us Pooh-Bahs of publishing. Gloster is out to show that when we in Christian publishing call our humble work a ministry, we are all too often out to hide our high-handed business tactics.

And these people know the worst: the boiler plate contracts that have steamed so many authors; basket royalty clauses—no picnic for a starving artist; "autobiographies" by best-selling "authors" that have been concocted by other hands (the "author" himself being unable to spell his name); the total lack of copyediting (a lost art form, alas, it's true); contracted books rejected because the latest marketing analysis says that the 32.5-year-old woman reader with three children and a Wagoneer is no longer interested in prayer; multiple-book contracts that find the publisher deliberately burying the books of a writer who is no longer in favor; celebrity authors who continue to be represented as spiritual giants when the publicity people on their author tours have to put them in straitjackets every night back at the hotel; the lamentable fact that most of the people in Christian publishing prefer to think of books as "units" and do not like to read (which, perhaps, it may be admitted, accounts for our somewhat condescending attitude toward writers); and the last guilty secret, we publishers hardly control the industry anymore, much less writers: we are all the servants of Pearl Harbor, Inc., the distribution company colossus.

Pearl Harbor now in effect determines our editorial policy because we cannot sell what Pearl Harbor does not distribute—most stores in the CBA market now order all their books from them. A great pity, and yet the Pooh-Bahs have not protested too much because, as all of us in Gloster's greedy group well know, through the subtleties of the discount game, Pearl Harbor costs us publishers nothing.

What are we to do? If all this were to become public, the public might protest, our audience become inattentive, our market mutiny!

Hastings looked up from his reading to Agatha, who was beginning to emerge as the possible murderer. She was pacing back and forth, putting her heels down with emphasis. Her chin slightly lifted, she was trying to brave out these moments, but the way she clasped her hands together let Hastings know she was praying for an unaccountable mercy.

He scanned through the next pages of the journal and watched the murder plot unfold. Whitewater had been particularly outraged that Gloster had the nerve to ask CURD to pay for the gathering, to put out a Mafia contract, in effect, on itself. If it had not been for CURD's mole at *Evangelism Today,* who had passed on to Whitewater FOR-YOUR-EYES-ONLY correspondence between Gloster and Yates, CURD, as Agatha herself had written, might have been curdled.

Gloster's ultimate ambition, one far surpassing the mere publication of *They Call It a Ministry,* finally determined the publisher's deathly course of action. The leading edge of Gloster's divide-and-conquer tactics, *They Call It a Ministry* would create a space the size of the Armageddon battlefield that he meant his own troops to occupy. With all of the established Christian publishers in disgrace, the writers themselves would form a publishing company, as Douglas Fairbanks, Mary Pickford, and Charlie Chaplin had founded United Artists long ago.

Gloster had in fact come up with his grand scheme, skimming through *Variety* at a kiosk on Rodeo Drive. (Out on one of his frequent speaking tours, he was practicing the ascetic discipline of window-shopping. Feel the temptation, he would later advise his vast audiences, experience the full horror of your own ego attachments, and let them go. Let them go now! Let them go utterly!)

The United Writers publishing company, like UA, would be founded of, for, and by the people most concerned with the industry's product, the writers themselves. It would be dedicated to serving them. And if he could get all the writers coming to Christhaven to give their new books to United Writers, his new publishing company would have a writers' stable second to none.

Gloster contacted Yates, Hastings had read, to enlist his cooperation as the editor of the proposed book. He wanted Yates to be president of the new company as well. (Gloster would be CEO.) Whitewater and Gaines thought they might limit themselves to killing Yates, since without his expertise,

Gloster could not possibly make the project work. (No matter how much money the other writers made, they were destined never to balance their checkbooks. And Gloster's ambitions, exalted as they might be, competed with his timidity for control of his actions: he was at heart an empire builder whose fears could always disguise themselves as humility, vaporizing the walls of the intended skyscraper in a moment, making the matter of his plans the stuff of dreams—rather like the Quaker notion of sacraments, a holy invisibility or nothingness, a reality too pure to exist.) Unfortunately, Yates had written to Adolphssohn and Stevens, asking their advice. He had also written to Hastings but for some reason had never sent the letter. *Holy crackers,* Hastings thought, *a first-class stamp from eternity!*

Hastings put away the journal and went over to Whitewater. He put his fingers to his neck and pressed down firmly at the carotid artery to feel any trace of pulse. The quondam publisher and former coconspirator was now most definitely dead.

"But this doesn't make sense," Hastings said to Agatha. "You didn't kill Whitewater."

"No."

"Is Emma Syss really here?"

"I'm not sure. I'm as puzzled about that as everyone else."

"But then what about Whitewater?"

"Bent. Well, not Bent."

"What?"

"Bent isn't Bent. I mean, his real name is Gerhardus Grossbuch."

"I never thought he was straight," Hastings said. "Actually, I never thought he was real. He struck me as the product of somebody's overly allegorical imagination."

"He was real enough. He's from Pearl Harbor, Inc."

"They know about this?"

"They know about everything."

Yes, Hastings thought, *that should have gone without saying.* He looked over at Yates, whose dead deadpan expression seemed to say, It's about time you caught on to the business side of things, dummy. "But what about you, Agatha? If Bent double-crossed Whitewater, you must be in danger."

"Who could I tell, though? I'd be sending myself to jail."

"People repent. People do all kinds of crazy things."

"I don't think Pearl Harbor believes in repentance."

"Mmm, probably not. Didn't you try to warn us, though, with your poem?"

"Agatha did."

"Agatha? You *are* Agatha. Aren't you?" *This is getting really creepy,* Hastings thought.

"It's like I'm two people," she said. "Agatha the poet. Gaines the publisher. That's why I've been such a yo-yo. I don't remember writing that poem—Gaines has been in control. Agatha has been trying to get out, though. She must have slipped out when Gaines wasn't looking—writing that poem."

"Sure, I understand," Hastings said, not really understanding at all.

"Out there in the snow when I threw up," Agatha said, "I think Gaines came out for good."

"But Bent or Grossbuch or whoever still isn't finished. We'd better get back to the others."

"Wait. There's a problem."

Hastings's look said he was well aware they had a number of problems.

"I mean, the others. They've been gassed."

"Are they dead?"

"Better than dead for Pearl Harbor's purposes. The gas brings on rapid mental deterioration and then total aphasia. They are not so slowly being deprived of their ability to use language."

"That would be Hell."

"That's what we had in mind," Agatha said, and gave a Gainesian grin despite herself.

S. J. marched up the last rise in the private road before it ran several hundred yards down to the lodge's doorstep. Night had nearly fallen. This Robin Redbreast of a man, with his prominent chest and quick, watchful eyes, had been out all day from the lodge, flying about the mountainside, looking for his wife, Magdalene. Although he wore a tweed jacket, having forgotten to bring a topcoat from New Orleans, the birdlike impression he made was so strong that, like Monsieur Poirot, he might have worn a swallow-tailed coat. Indeed, among the Christhaven writers, S. J. was the most likely person to play the decorous inquisitor, Hercule. His manners were those of the New York literary establishment; manners akin to a fencer's, poised and arched like the fencer's trailing hand and yet as swift as an épée to parry and thrust. He knew how to despatch an opponent. He had a voice that glided and ran like a woodwind instrument of a fine articulation, with piccolo flourishes of laughter. In his discreet behavior he was as polished as the lenses of his tortoiseshell reading glasses; a gentleman whose social graces were but the visible signs of modestly concealed virtues. He sometimes worked at an analogous task, as well, employing his powers of deduction as an investigative reporter, detecting the foibles and follies of religious publishing for *Publishers Weekly*.

S. J. did not rush out to find Magdalene when she was discovered missing because he thought he knew where she was. She had remarked on what an ideal hermitage the uppermost cabin above the lodge would make, and he presumed she had gone there, well before dawn, to meditate.

Magdalene arose habitually at 4 A.M., like a discalced Carmelite, to say matins. S. J. had not voiced his suspicions as to her whereabouts to the others because he wanted to find her first, in order to explain about his night in the women's room.

They had had enough trouble with that kind of thing already: the cause of Magdalene's late distress and their marital squabbles had been Johns's attentions to Felicity French. As this love triangle became a quadrangle, Magdalene wanted to square things by lopping S. J.'s hands off.

They had been married for so long that he had not minded, until now, his wife's epistolary affair with the poet—they had fondled nothing but each other's stationery. Her attraction to Johns had recalled to Magdalene the dearness of the flesh when she was far too apt to wish herself gone from the body and this life of worldly pain. It had given S. J. the chance to play the wise and forbearing spouse, the prophet calling his wayward bride back to fidelity. He had reached almost messianic heights in his condescension to his own Mary Magdalene. The affair had, in a phrase, put him one up on her for the very first time in their years together, and he had enjoyed the leverage it gave him.

Johns's hanging about Felicity had spoiled the delicate balance on which that leverage depended. Magdalene had begun upbraiding her husband for his inadequacies, taking her anger at Johns out on him! (She may have been paying him back for a little cookie he had dallied with long ago in New York, although he found a revenge enacted twenty years after the fact too de Maupassant to credit.) He had had a moment or two last night in which he had almost wished the killer might elect Magdalene as his next victim.

But S. J. had become alarmed when Magdalene had not returned by midmorning. He had gone to the cabin first, of course, finding nothing. After returning to the lodge at noon to eat, he had recommenced the search that afternoon.

As he looked up from his weary path through the snow, he saw Agatha and Hastings walking down from the cabins to the lodge. He waved to them in greeting. Hastings made a much more urgent gesture in reply, windmilling his arm for S. J. to cross whatever danger zone lay between them.

The younger author began to mush through the snow toward S. J., with Agatha hurrying to catch up. He actually dived across the last few paces against the older man's chest, clinging for a moment to S. J. by the lapels. "Don't go in there!" he screamed. He took several heaving breaths and then said in a rasping voice, modulated as if he did not want the surrounding trees to overhear, "We have to talk first."

Hastings is a one-man opera, S. J. thought ruefully, but followed him to the side of the lodge for a confab with Agatha. Soon Hastings and Agatha brought him up to speed, telling him about finding the bodies in the cabin. (They weren't there when he had visited the cabin earlier in the day.)

"But where's Magdalene, then?" S. J. asked. "And why Magdalene?"

Agatha wouldn't say.

"Perhaps Whitewater or Grossbuch came upon her accidentally when she went out to pray. Maybe he thought of using her as bait."

The terrible thing is, every once in a while the younger writer almost makes sense, S. J. thought.

"Anyway, we have to get inside and help the others now."

"*Can* we help them?" S. J. asked. The two men looked at Agatha. "Is there an antidote?"

"I'm sure there must be," Agatha said. "I mean, I don't know much about it. Even Grossbuch didn't quite understand the gas."

"Tell us what you do know," S. J. said.

"It's called Nemein 3. I didn't want to use it at first. But Grossbuch convinced Whitewater and me that it wouldn't be enough to stop Gloster's new publishing company. After spending time with the writers' group, Grossbuch thought that any one of us might eventually compose something like *They Call It a Ministry.* He said he had never heard such bitching."

"Nemein 3," S. J. said, musing. "Nemein 3."

"How could you have gotten involved in this?" Hastings

asked, his voice exasperated, his soul chilled.

Agatha was desperate to be understood. "I told you. Agatha wasn't in control—Gaines was in control. And Gaines thought that as the writers went *non compos mentis*, she could get them all to sign over their reprint rights to her. Gaines Godly would have had a backlist second to none."

Hastings rolled his eyes. "Holy crackers," he said. "We'd better get in there and try to do something!"

For once, S. J. entirely agreed.

Entering the lodge, they expected to find a cuckoo's nest. Instead, Gloster had the group arranged in a circle for discussion before the flaming hearth. The wood, which had been retrieved from the pile on the damp balcony, hissed and popped.

"Come, join us, come be among us," Gloster said, falling into the literature-in-translation diction he used when nervously exercising authority. "We're talking about our future writing projects."

"Magdalene!" S. J. cried. "Thank God." He went over to her, clasped her around the neck, and gave her several hard kisses on the lips, an unusual display of emotion for S. J. Smith. "Where have you been?"

"Heaven," she said. She laughed. "I'm not kidding, I'll tell you about it. Sit down."

"I'm sure you'll want to go over all that later," Gloster said, dismissing the reunion of the Smiths. "Wesley, why don't you go next," he said. He glanced at each member of the tardy trio. "We want to know what you all are going to be doing after you leave here."

S. J. found this congenial parley in the midst of crisis more than bizarre, but then these people were largely Evangelicals and they had so little place for the tragic in their theology that they were bound, on principle, to overlook it. Still, he wanted to get away and talk with Magdalene. He put his arm around her shoulders and pulled her to him. She looked up at him, suddenly frightened, her eyes glaring and colorless, as if he were a stranger accosting her on the street. He touched her cheek, cupping her jaw. She melted—as quickly as she had become frightened—into randyness: one corner of her mouth hitched up like a hooker's sassy buttock, her eyes half-closed and rheumy with passion. Something was very wrong.

"Well, friend," Wesley said, "I don't remember what I was going to do, but one heck of a great idea just came to me. How about a biblical novel based on the life of Eutychus—the man who falls out of the window when the apostle Paul is preaching? We'd see in exquisitely researched detail what has brought this miserable character to the place where he falls out the window, and then we would see how his whole life is changed by virtue of that one snooze."

"Ooooohhhhh," Shirley squealed, "that's so exciting. I can track with that." She hurried on with her speech, keeping the floor. "I have a new idea, too. How about a book on Christian dentistry? The Bible has a lot to say about teeth. The psalmist is always asking the Lord to break somebody's."

"I've always wanted to do a book—I hope you don't mind me jumping in here," Gloster said. "I've always wanted to do a book in which I could write about all the people I've ever heard of I didn't like and link them all to the Devil through a conspiracy theory. Maybe the theory would be that they use their imaginations. That could be it. Everybody's guilty of using his imagination!"

Magdalene fingered S. J.'s collar. She ran her hand up the side of his neck into his fluffy silver hair. Without turning to look at the others, keeping her eyes on her hubby, she said, "I'd like to do a Christian sex manual. The Bible is full of sex. All kinds of it. Good sex. Bad sex. What do you think, Sammy? Goooood sex or baaaaad sex?"

Lynne Teal jumped into the conversation. "I never really thought about writing a book before. But being with this group the past two days has made me think that just about anybody can write a book." She stopped, looked around. Everyone was still smiling stupidly at her. "I'd write about the higher critics in biblical studies, especially the redactionists, and I'd show that their methods are evil because their conclusions are evil and that's all because they are evil people. It would be called *The Response of the Ostrich.*"

Johns said, "I want to do Christian revisions of the classic fairy tales. No big bad wolves in mine. No way. Everything will be sweetness and light. Sweetness and light and la de dah de dah." He paused and thought a moment, rolling his head back. He looked for all the world as if he had just been shot full of Demerol. "La de dah de dah," he said. "La de dah de dah." He started clapping to the rhythm. "La de dah de dah." Clap. "La de dah de dah," clap clap. Soon the other book proposers were clapping and joining in with him, "La de dah de dah."

S. J. saw the no-more-than-usually-insane Hastings rolling his eyes, circling his index finger by his ear, his tongue lolling out of his mouth. S. J. motioned for the madman and Agatha to retreat with him. The others were too caught up in their singsong chant to care about their departure.

Downstairs, by the Ping-Pong table, late the scene of Philippa and Agatha's marvelous match, the three held a last breathless conference.

"How about running for our lives," Hastings said. "Let's get out of here."

"Hastings," S. J. said disapprovingly. Then he spoke in his usual lighthearted tone once more. "If memory serves," he said, looking away into the distance of his own thoughts, "*nemein* is a Greek verb meaning to distribute. It's the root from which we get *nemesis.*"

"Nemesis." Agatha said. "Emma Syss." She paused, thinking. "I'm not sure what this has to do with the gas, but I had the idea that Philippa was going through something like I was. A case of split personality. Maybe Philippa needed an emetic for her own personal bogeyman."

"Her experience could have been a kind of premonition," S. J. said, enigmatically. "She is a contemporary prophet."

"What are you talking about?" Hastings asked.

S. J. did not reply directly, feeling no need to make Hastings privy to his deepest thoughts. He needed him to carry out a task, though. "Look, Hastings," he said, "if you are worried about the danger, why don't you see if you can find Philippa's gun."

Hastings replied with his best sneer, which on his boyish face looked more like a comical grimace—the expression of a three year old playing Al Capone—and then left on his appointed task. S. J. asked himself, *Which would you rather have, a son who readily agrees to do what you ask and never does, or one who refuses and then goes ahead? The Lord might have a spot in his heart yet for Hastings.*

When S. J. turned to discuss the matter with Agatha, he found that her attention had wandered to the singsong chant, which continued from above. She was swaying, taking jab steps, and swinging her head back and forth with the lah de dahs. She had her palms cupped together as if she might begin clapping with the group above at the next rhythmic punctuation.

"Agatha," S. J. said.

"I was thinking," she said. "I was thinking that for my next project I would like to do a series of poems that you wouldn't have to think about twice. You know the kind of thing? I'm tired of poetry with deep meanings, aren't you? I think it's time for something light, something lighter than air." She giggled, and then, as if lighter than air herself, floated up the stairs.

S. J. had worried that Grossbuch had planned to double-cross Agatha as well as Whitewater, and he now saw that the self-administered half-dose she had received of Nemein 3, although it had taken longer to have its effect, was working its same degenerative evil in her.

Mixed with the rhythmic clapping from the first floor came an ill-timed half-stroke, which grew and expanded into the methodically abusive buffeting of a helicopter, its wash eventually encircling the lodge, draining all else into its whirlpool. S. J. ran back upstairs to the group.

He arrived to find Bent, AKA. Grossbuch, with two accomplices, goons in white hospital uniforms, standing on the outside of the writers' circle, before the bay window. One of the goons was tall, with a cone-shaped neck and a head as flat as an eraser; the other was a wide-body, his arms so short that he looked as if he might not be able to join his hands together in front of his chest. Grossbuch was now wearing a cowboy getup: fringed leather jacket, plaid shirt, string tie with its turquoise clasp. He also wore a pair of gold-rimmed spectacles, which reflected the light from the wagon wheel chandelier above when he glanced upward, making him, it seemed, impervious to Heavenly influences, blind. S. J. noticed that Hastings had beaten him back to the writers' circle and had taken a seat among the others.

"Where you been, S. J.?" Grossbuch said. "These people are in a heap of trouble. I seen where this was headed and I recruited some fellers from the local hospital. We'd better get them along to the docs."

"You can cut the Marshall Dillon act, Grossbuch," S. J. said. "Agatha talked before the gas got to her."

The lean-faced man looked over at Agatha, who had her legs tucked up to one side of her chair and a look on her face of ever-shifting amazement. Grossbuch noted the change in her with a clinical detachment. "She . . . vas . . . so . . . gullipill," he said in an exaggerated Nazi accent.

"She was a writer," S. J. said. Grossbuch put his hand to his mouth and appeared to laugh. "It's true," S. J. said, "all writers are about six years old emotionally. They have to be.

They are called by the Lord to remain open to the world with a childlike innocence. It is their burden and their gift."

"Dese wrrrituhs are innosunt?"

"They trust their perceptions, as children do."

"Putt dey hate each utter for effery reason imaginaple."

"No they don't."

"De prose writuhs hate de puh-etz, de nonfickshuhn writuhs hate de fickshuhn writuhs, de realistick fickshun writuhs hate de fantuhcists. Und vizah-vuhsah. Vuts more, de Prahtessstuhntz hate de Cattuhlicks. Und vizah-vuhsah. Nein. Dese writuhs are und knot of vipuss, und ssssnakepit."

S. J. knew there was some justice in this.

"I tink at fust ve pin de murtuhs on Glostah," Grossbuch said. "A leetle frame-up jop. Den, I say no. Dese writuhs, all de writuhs, are devils. Dey are zo much kanzer und de broderhood. Dey must be puriefite!

"I zee dat iss zo. I see da Lord's peepul vill not be safe undill dese devils be exorcised. So ve haf de Nemein Tree. It iss, as you say, und metaphor uf hour verk at Pearl Harbor, Ink. It cleanses de temple of Gott uf dese devils. It purifites bad thoughts from da mind. It iss like emetick dat purifites za potty. Vitout dese writuhs de broderhoot vill be clean again."

"Why didn't you gas me?" S. J. asked.

"You are reporter for *Pooblishers Veekly,* jah? You tell de peepul vut has happen. How George Glostah has foolet dese peepul, dese wrrrituhs, into New Age channeling. So dey go crazy, jah? Dey loose der minden. You tell peepul dis and maybe Pearl Harbor vill distribute your pooks. Uttervise you never sell a pook again."

Hastings began to act like one of those sad mental patients who has taken too much Thorazine, flicking his tongue out of his mouth again and again, a lizard on an insect-rich evening. He was also drooling, his saliva coming off his chin in long, elastic threads.

Some of the other writers were well into their own infantile regressions. Johns and Felicity had their arms clasped around each other's necks and were sucking each other's thumbs; Willer had plopped down on all fours and like a Brobdingnagian infant was trying to take a nap with his bottom in the air.

Only Philippa, forceful soul that she was, seemed to be resisting the influence of the gas. She sat with a terrible calm, looking straight ahead. Behind her steadfast gaze, she seemed to be noting every minute change in her frame of mind; and yet deep within her focused attention there seemed horror as well, for ordinarily she would have been making these mental notes about her cognitions in order to write about the same; and yet her self-consciousness told her that writing was precisely what she would never be able to do again.

Gloster looked panic-stricken. He had his hands at his beard as if this growth had come upon him as inexplicably as ass's ears on King Midas.

"Ve haf dese yackets vitout sleeves," Grossbuch said, holding up a straitjacket as if it were a visual aid in a Sunday school class. "Ve vunt all de kinden to putz zem on und come haf der kaffeee klatch in ze hosspitle. Jah? Das iss goot idea, I tink."

Hastings stood and walked toward Grossbuch.

Absolutely true to his precipitate surname, without any clumsy motions that might have clued Grossbuch to Hastings's true intentions, not delaying his purpose in the slightest even to build the dramatic tension and heighten our pleasure in reading, but with a motion so swift that S. J.'s rush of adrenalin at its anticipation failed to speed his heart rate before its execution, Hastings whipped Philippa's revolver to within a centimeter of Grossbuch's temple and blew the man's sweetmeats against the shattering bay window behind him. Grossbuch's brain matter ran down what was left of the window as if it had been composed of raw eggs.

The goons turned to seize him, and Hastings shot them in the heart. One! Two! They fell backward and hit the floor, thump, bodies so dense that they neither bounced nor settled, sacks of concrete tossed onto a loading platform.

"What have I done?" Hastings cried, clutching his head in his hands. He fell to the floor and groveled there, absurdly penitent.

"Hastings, Harold, please, get up," said S. J. "You did well." And he bent down and clasped Hastings above the elbow, hoisting him to his feet.

"I haven't had a fight since I was in fourth grade," Hastings said, boohooing out the words.

"You have now," S. J. said.

The two paused for a moment together and gradually became aware of the other writers, looking up to them from the cowering positions they had taken on the floor when Hastings's shots rang out.

Philippa alone remained in her chair. There was the slightest pinch between her brows, as if she could barely remember that there was something she must remember, and yet, clearly, she did not know why she should remember it any longer.

"Let's get out of here," Hastings said. "We can send back a real medical team and the police."

"It's dark as pitch outside," S. J. said. Now that night had fallen, the clouds that had come up in the late afternoon blocked any trace of starlight. "Anyway, I have an idea. Help me arrange our friends in another circle. Not on the chairs. Just help me get them into a ring on the floor. Philippa too. I don't want her to be hurt."

"Give me a moment," Hastings said. S. J. found that he too needed to recollect himself. Rarely had justice been executed so swiftly—a murderer and his cohorts judged and executed at nearly the same moment. Whitewater, too, had paid for his sins. The police might want to talk with Agatha, but he thought she would be cleared by reason of insanity—if they could only find a way to help their colleagues.

S. J. pulled back the writers' chairs while Hastings helped his benumbed friends to their places along the periphery of the hooked rug in the middle of the room. They looked, in their discombobulated state, as dull as old stones ringing a campfire. They were totally oblivious to the presence of the dead. *The spark that might make these stones glow,* S. J. thought, *that might make them living stones again in the City of God, would have to fall upon them from above.*

"You'd better sit down as well, Hastings," S. J. said.

He raised both hands, palms outward, in a hieratic gesture of summoning. "*In nomine patris, filii, et spiritus sancti,*" S. J. said, and both men antiphoned amen as they crossed themselves.

> "Hail Holy Light, offspring of Heav'n firstborn,
> Bright effluence of bright essence increate!"

S. J. paused, not quite sure how to continue.

"Who once didst inspire the shepherd prophet king, Jesse's poet son, and blessed your apostle with a vision of the third heaven; who instructed your servant on Patmos to write what he saw. . . ."

S. J. paused again, surprised and delighted with his own eloquence—not a bad impromptu invocation; it gave him a number of totally inappropriate ideas about future projects. He raised his hands a little higher and continued.

"See these thy servants, dreamers of dreams and singers of songs—soothsayers who like St. John Chrysostom have spoken with the golden tongues of angels, almost always with charity. At least pretty much. Take pity on these creatures of words who, like fictional characters, would be nothing without them. And by all that is holy, the common word exact without vulgarity, the formal word precise but not pedantic, the complete consort dancing together; and invoking the aid of St. Augustine, St. Shakespeare, St. Pascal, St. Dostoevsky, St. Mark Twain, St. T. S. Eliot, St. Flannery O'Connor, and William Faulkner, the Venerable, whose works continually give you praise, I pray that you would create them anew. For this is always your will. . . .

"But, as we know, we wrestle not against flesh and blood, but against syntax and diction. And therefore, in the firm belief that in giving humankind language, you distinguished us from the beasts, gave us the wealth of the soul, and that any force which dulls that coinage must also tarnish and obscure the stamp it bears, your image; believing that you communicate with us and that communication proceeds most especially through words and therefore that any force, agency, institution, publishing company, distribution company, or spirit which dulls, degrades, or destroys language cannot be of you; I command the unholy spirits possessing our friends and colleagues, devils whose spirits Pearl Harbor, Inc., has distributed amongst them, and any devils which may have invaded their souls by whatsoever means. . . .

"I command these linguistic oppressors, all you minions of Satan, to name yourselves and to depart from among us. Return to the pit of the inarticulate, the swamp of the banal, the mire of the mundane, the lake of the loquacious, the inferno of the periphrastic, and the lowest ring of the risible from whence you come and be known no more in our midst!"

For a moment . . . silence. Then S. J. and Hastings both became aware of a hissing sound. They turned to the fire to see whether a last wet log were catching. But the fire had long gone out. The hissing became more intense, and with it there came a buzzing, as if a coil of snakes had decided to make its nest in a beehive and the two species had found themselves engaged in unlikely combat.

Then there came an explosive popping. S. J. looked back to the fire, but already he knew it could not be the source of these volatile reports. The hissing and the buzzing rose once more, and then came another popping explosion, and this time S. J. saw a kind of air bubble, like the thought of a cartoon character, appear above Willer's head and whisk off into the night. Before he knew it there were more explosions.

Asterisks and ampersands arose into the air. The asterisks made the hissing sounds, the ampersands buzzed. Copyright insignia; exclamation marks; dollar, pound, and percentage signs joined them, twirling about each other in a witch's circle about level with the wagon wheel chandelier. Then these dancing figures all sped out, through the blasted window, into the night.

Strange groaning belches erupted next, the hiccups of the nether world, like gases from decaying beasts boiling through slime or tar. These belches lengthened into basso profundo groanings. Voices of decay and desolation seemed about to speak, but their low-throated protests remained strangled. The groanings became louder until they finally roared out their distress, the affliction lodged in their very names.

A groan like a Sandi Patti album played backward came from Shirley. She was thrown forward from her knees to a prone position on the floor. A sprite popped out of her mouth as she fell. It was shaped like a hair curler and called itself HARLEQUIN ROMANCE.

The convulsions in Gloster's chest disgorged a rainbowlike being, who called itself WITCH HUNT before departing.

Strangely, since he had not been gassed, an evil spirit emerged from Hastings as well. It blew out from his mouth in a cloud of octopussical ink, howling its terrible name: CRITICISM.

One by one the authors groaned, retched, and collapsed in a dead faint. The slurred roarings of the voices knocked the permaplaque Scriptures off the walls and sucked the air out of the holy whoopee cushions. The demonic energies ignited the "No Smoking" signs. The springs and balance wheels of the woodchopper cuckoo clock exploded, and the little woodsman came out of his hut and buried his ax in his own thigh. (The chimes of the clock would never again play "Just As I Am" but changed their tune to "For All the Saints, Who from Their Labors Rest.") The lodge stood; but the Jesus junk fried.

Devils named TREACLY VERSE, PARANOID PROPHECY, MINDLESS LITERALISM, REACTIONARY POLITICS, IDOLATROUS BIBLICISM, and GENRE FICTION, those fabulous oppressors of language whose corrupt sensibilities had undone so many, confessed themselves and vanished.

Truly, S. J. thought, Pearl Harbor, Inc., had unleashed the bottom of the pit against them.

A creature like a troll doll wrapped in a fur coat came out of Philippa, calling itself EMMA SYSS. And there were other, more common demons, who called themselves DELUSIONS OF GRANDEUR, MIDNIGHT TOIL, VAUNTED AMBITION, and MEGALOMANIA.

Finally S. J. himself, having experienced a rending and pointed hauling in his stomach, the uncoiling of a trot line heavy with treble hooks, slumped to his knees. A terrible creature was slashing its way out of his throat. As last he coughed up what proved to be a two-dimensional being, with the laminated look and credit card proportions of a press pass, which called itself JOURNALISM as it whiffled into the night. All was still. They all slept.

Gloster awoke in a prone position, half-kneeling, his nose mashed into the hooked rug. He wondered what madness had led him to resume pronal meditation, and then he remembered where he was, at Christhaven, and what had gone on, the murders. The mantle of guilt he had carried ever since Nathaniel Yates turned up dead on the trestle table descended upon him once more. He felt especially guilty because he knew he was ambivalent about the murderer's discovery.

His plan for *They Call It a Ministry* and United Writers looked, in the black light of the murders, like an eerily glowing poster of his own ambition. Ambition! It rose up within him like Jack's beanstalk. And so often when he laid into it with the ax of ascetical practice he found that he was only trying to bring the giant's castle down to his own level.

He raised his head and looked around him. A scene like a bunch of toadstools underneath swaying fronds swam before his eyes. As his vision focused, he realized the toadstools were the other writers, each in his or her own pronal crouch, the fronds the seats of straight-backed chairs. What had happened?

"Aaaaaggghhh." Someone was groaning. "Aaaaagggh," the sound came again. Gloster looked over to see S. J. struggling to his feet. The hoary-headed man rocked back on his heels and attempted to propel himself to his full height. He looked like a weight lifter performing an incredibly sloppy clean and jerk.

Gloster found his own feet and went over to S. J. He noticed that the others were coming around as well.

"That'll teach me to hang around with Evangelicals," S. J. said. "Enthusiasm, thy name is heresy. But what a rush!"

"What happened?" Gloster asked. "Do you know?" Then he had a thought. "Is everyone here? No one else—" and then he saw Grossbuch. "Oh, no!" Gloster cried. "Not Bent! Not—" And then he saw the goons. "Who are these other people?" His tone had changed to annoyance. "What in the world is going on?"

"I think I'd better explain it to everybody," S. J. said. "Help me get the others back to their chairs. Let's see what kind of shape we're in."

As they recovered from the exorcism, the writers realized they had returned to consciousness none too soon, as the cold the broken window had let in had nearly resulted in a pandemic of hypothermia.

S. J., Willer, and Hastings lit a veritable blaze in the hearth. Johns and Felicity snuggled together once again. Magdalene, Philippa, Agatha, Shirley, and Lynne brought down blankets from the bedrooms above as wraps. Gloster busied himself with worrying over the window. Johns and Felicity finally came to his aid: they unclasped long enough to retrieve a cardboard box and tape from the kitchen. Together the three repaired the window. Flattened out, the box covered the empty space, although a thermal aneurysm threatened with every pulse of the wind.

Hastings took it upon himself to drag Grossbuch and his goons outside. "These spies," he said, "will never come in from the cold."

The others turned to S. J. for an explanation. He gave them a rundown.

"But how did you think to perform an exorcism?" Willer asked.

"I can't believe this," Hastings interpolated. "We're not going to have the scene where Sherlock explains the information the author has kept privileged along with his own incredibly astute deductions. Please. Tell me we're not."

Somewhere Mabel Stevens was thinking: *You hate anything but the type of thing you do, Hastings.* She was right.

"Hastings has his point," Johns said. "I, too, become a little uneasy when life imitates art too closely."

"Would you all please shut up," Shirley said, her voice becoming ever more girlish as it rose. "Let S. J. explain."

"The name of the gas, as it happens, gave me my most significant clue," S. J. said, assuming a professorial manner. "It was called Nemein 3." As he continued, his training in the scholastics came to the fore; he proceeded through a philological rooting out of the mystery's etiology, in the best Aristotelian style. "*Nemein* is the Greek verb *to distribute.* And

Grossbuch described the gas as a metaphor for the work of the distributor. He even said that we were like unclean thoughts or spirits within the mind of the Christian world.

"Now," S. J. said, continuing, "as we know from St. Thomas, evil is always a counterfeit of the good, a present absence, a privation of being. And what Nemein 3 was distributing among us was the absence of language—a positive negativity, an evil. The Greek verb *nemein* is the basis of our word *nemesis,* the distribution of retributive justice, usually, as we use it, through a persistent opponent. *Nemein* is closely related to the Greek verb *emein,* from which we get *emesis* or *vomiting.* In many exorcisms the exit of the demons occasions disgorgement or retching."

"Was that what happened to me?" Agatha asked.

"I don't think so," S. J. said. "Split personality is a phenomenon quite distinct from demon possession. Yet your sense of Agatha escaping the tyranny of Gaines did prompt my thinking.

"Your experience, Philippa, was key." S. J. went on. "Emma Syss does exist. She is a devil, who I believe has inhabited other bodies as well as your own during our stay here at Christhaven. Since your work serves a prophetic function in so many peoples' lives, articulating their experience and enabling them to go forward with you in their spiritual journeys, I thought that you might, in your encounters with Emma Syss, be experiencing a foreshadowing of what we all came to know, demon possession."

At that moment a huge Balkan woman in a fur coat crossed the hearth room, nodded severely to the group, and entered the pool enclosure.

"What time is it?" Lynne asked.

"Five fifteen, A.M." Magdalene said. "I should be at my matins."

"And if I had accepted Grossbuch's premises," S. J. said, his voice lower but projected with more force to recapture the group's attention, "if I had accepted Grossbuch's premises, that we are the evil ones, I might have been inclined to see his Nemein 3 as the agent of our necessary emesis from the body.

"I am no Romantic," S. J. said. (No one had ever accused him of being one, surely.) "Nor a dualist. I know the heart, even the heart of a writer, is desperately wicked. But the truly redemptive act is an act of self-emptying, self-willed renunciation. In fact, our Lord's own sacrifice is described by that same word *emein.* And he came to bring not retributive justice—that, after all, is the law—but grace. He is not our nemesis but our advocate."

"If this gets any more theological," Hastings murmured, "our story is going to take on the dimensions of a fairy tale."

"I think we are already well into the land of faerie," Johns said. "You yourself, Hastings, are as weird as any weird sister ever was."

"Be that as it may," S. J. said. "As I was saying, given our Lord's own action of self-emptying, I had to think that Grossbuch's means of purification was wrong. At the same time, remembering that evil is a counterfeit of the good, I wondered if his thoughts might be suggestive of the virtue or power that we needed to undo the evil of the gas. Thus I came up with the idea of the exorcism."

"I detect something distinctly allegorical going on here," Hastings said.

Johns agreed. "For example," he said, "isn't it significant that Bent turns out to be Gerhardus Grossbuch, not merely a German but a cartoon Nazi?"

"What do you mean?" Shirley asked.

"I think I know," Magdalene said. "There are very few stock characters available as villains any more. We are supposed to have a global, nonnationalistic consciousness, and so you can't project national hatreds in developing antagonists."

"With one exception," Philippa said. "The Germans. More

specifically, the Nazis."

"Right," Magdalene said. "The Nazis are the only people you can hate unashamedly. You can't hate the Russians because they are 'another competing nation state with their own legitimate interests in our pluralistic world.'"

"What about the Japanese?" Felicity asked. "Grossbuch represented Pearl Harbor, Inc."

"It's okay," Willer said, "to refer to Pearl Harbor because that recalls a day of imperialistic infamy. But you can't hate the Japanese anymore because *we* dropped the bomb on *them.*"

"Wait a minute," Gloster said, feeling as if his writers' meeting were degenerating into a lit. crit. session. "What are you all talking about?"

"Life imitating art," Johns said.

"You call this life?" Hastings asked, and finally got a laugh out of the group.

"The real problem," Johns said, "is with S. J.'s analysis itself. Don't you think you kind of finessed that one, S. J.?"

"It's not my chapter," S. J. said.

"Well, who did write this chapter?" Shirley asked.

Johns worked his lips as if tasting a wine that he was finding had already started to turn to vinegar and then delivered his verdict. "Someone who has read far too much Barth and Barthelme."

"Someone with a deeply paranoid view of the world," Agatha said. "Have you noticed the us-them mentality in this thing?"

"What I want to know," Shirley said, "is why Agatha said Nathaniel's *It Hurts When It Hurts* undercut her publishing house's *The Popularity of Pain,* when Wesley said that *It Hurts When It Hurts* hadn't come out yet."

"And who was the one chanting *Kyrie, eleison?*" Magdalene asked.

"And why was the killer identified with the words *Et tu,*

Brute by one of his victims?" Philippa asked. She was especially interested in this question, as she often introduced famous quotes into her own work.

"For that matter," Lynne said, "who tied Felicity up?"

"Oh gosh," Felicity said. "I know this sounds silly." She looked down, as if she were silently asking permission of the panting hart on her sweater to reveal their secret. "I tied myself up. I was hoping Livy would find me. I thought we might . . . play. You know, bondage."

"It's easy enough to lay bare this text," Hastings said.

"And yet," said Johns, who, like Hastings, could find no real forgiveness as a writer for the terrible knowledge he had acquired as a scholar, "and yet the underlying motivations seem to have been divined and exploited to considerable effect."

Gloster thought he would go mad. The propensity of his peers to observe their own existence and quarrel over its interpretation from moment to moment tempted him to mix his own batch of Nemein 3. He had had such great plans for this writers' gathering, and now he saw that even if a number of the writers had not been knocked off, still the occasion most probably would have come to nought. Writers would fight about anything. Trying to get a bunch of writers together for a single purpose was like trying to form a union of anarchists!

The inevitable onslaught of the meaning of meaning finally assailed Gloster as well. All things work to the good, the Scriptures say. What good could he find in these days at Christhaven? And if none were to be found, did he still love the Lord? His own motivations, he feared, had been riddled with unholy ambition. He had even had the temerity to ask CURD to pay to help set up its own competition. And as a result three of his fellow writers were dead. And yet even if he had not made this critical mistake, would anything have been accomplished? He was nearly in despair.

"Saint Denis be my guide," Johns exclaimed, aptly alluding

to Hamlet.

For there before them, as if in answer to Gloster's shudderings of the spirit, arose a vision. It appeared among them as suddenly and contextually as white plumes of breath on a cold day. It seemed to have been there all along like moisture in the air and then to have suddenly condensed into palpable form. There, before them, Yates, Adolphssohn, and Stevens appeared in the parlor of a very Edwardian sort of Heaven, dressed in tweeds, seated in wingback chairs. They were reading from a book that they passed from hand to hand. Adolphssohn pointed to a passage with the stem of his cold pipe and read it out to the others, at which they all commenced to laugh. The book seemed to be some sort of preposterous, and probably highly literary, joke. The vision had a grainy texture and faded in and out, the figures appearing, growing more distinct, and then moving away like sheets of rain in a heavy storm.

"I can't believe this," Hastings said, "a *deus ex machina*."

"Yes," Philippa said, "and a universalist *deus ex machina*. Look!"

Behind the seated figures a man with gold-rimmed spectacles, a saberlike nose, and cowboy boots approached through the mists. Two fellows, one tall and lean, one very wide, walked behind him. They were coming to join in on the reading. The vision wafted in and out of view and at last faded away.

The writers debated what the vision meant. And for once they nearly came to consensus on the matter. The vision, they concluded, must have represented God's view of their Christhaven sojourn.

The writers came to believe that God must, after all, have had a purpose in bringing them together, despite the tragedy of their friends' deaths. This purpose had to do with producing a testimony, maybe something like a book, a most unusual, nay, almost unimaginable, book, which would detail their concerns for the state of their industry in disguised form. This testimony would urge the writers themselves to purify their own envious and quarrelsome natures, while it registered their concerns about their industry with the public.

Some of the writers believed that on the cover of the book they saw the title *Semper Reformanda*, which, being interpreted, means, "always be reforming." The title, these members said, suggested that religious publishing, like all things human, needs to examine its conscience.

Others thought that *Semper Reformanda* was a very strange title for a funny book. They noted how happy their compatriots had looked and how amused they had been by the book they were reading. They saw their Heavenly colleagues' laughter as the book's only message. The laughter of their friends they took to be one with the divine laughter: the delight God takes in his creatures, who, believing themselves on a metaphysical battlefield, are sometimes merely under the big top, performing their aerial gymnastics off the flying trapeze for pleasure.

At any rate, all the writers agreed that the book was a symbol of God's mysterious ways, his baffling providence, and only those mysterious ways could finally account for the carnage at Christhaven.

OMEGA

ABOUT THE AUTHORS

HAROLD FICKETT is the author of *The Holy Fool,* a novel, and *Flannery O'Connor: Images of Grace,* a critical biography. He is co-editor of *Image: A Journal of Religion and the Arts* and a fellow of The Milton Center at Friends University.

RICHARD J. FOSTER is executive director of the Milton Center at Friends University in Wichita, where he is professor of theology and writer in residence. He is author of *Celebration of Discipline, Freedom of Simplicity,* and *Money, Sex & Power.*

EMILIE GRIFFIN, a writer on conversion and prayer, sometime advertising copywriter and theology student, lives with her husband, William, in New Orleans. She is the author of *Turning: Reflections on the Experience of Conversion* and *Clinging: The Experience of Prayer,* as well as a book on the spiritual path called *Chasing the Kingdom.* She has written and coproduced a twelve-part television series on the Bible, "Understanding God's Word."

WILLIAM GRIFFIN, an editor at Macmillan and Harcourt for twenty years, now resides in New Orleans, where he is religious books editor of *Publishers Weekly;* he is author of, among other books, *Clive Staples Lewis: A Dramatic Life* and *The Fleetwood Correspondence: An Epistolary Novel.*

ALICE SLAIKEU LAWHEAD's writings include *The Christmas Book* and *The Lie of the Good Life;* with her husband Steve she has coauthored *The Ultimate Student Handbook* and *Pilgrim's Guide to the New Age.* An inveterate collector of quips and quotes, she actually enjoys writers' conferences.

STEPHEN R. LAWHEAD, often accused of harboring the demon of Genre Fiction, is the author of numerous science fiction and fantasy titles, most notable of which is the three-volume *Pendragon Cycle.*

MADELINE L'ENGLE is the author of more than forty books for readers of all ages, including the 1963 Newbery Medal winner, *A Wrinkle in*

Time. Her most recent publication, *Two Part Invention—The Story of a Marriage,* is the fourth in the autobiographical series, *The Crosswick Journals.* Traveling widely from her home base in New York, she lectures at writers' conferences and addresses church and student groups in the U.S. and abroad.

KAREN BURTON MAINS has found herself (sometimes by means of duress) involved in various forms of communication. She cohosts with her husband, David, the national radio daily "The Chapel of the Air." A conference teacher, her work ranges from social issues such as child abuse *(Child Sexual Abuse: A Hope for Healing)* to children's stories *(Tales of The Kingdom, Tales of the Resistance).* Since writing "In the Women's Room," she hasn't slept well.

CALVIN MILLER, pastor of Westside Baptist Church in Omaha for twenty-three years, has published a trilogy of fantasy novels called *The Singreale Chronicles* as well as an autobiographical account of the writing of his sonnets, *If This Be Love.* His *Singer Trilogy* has been popular for fifteen years in the Christian marketplace. He suspects many prominent Christians have unconfessed tattoos, and his contribution to *Carnage* deals with this deception.

LUCI SHAW, president of Harold Shaw Publishers in Wheaton, Illinois, has been writer-in-residence at several universities in the United States and Canada. She conceived and edited the Wheaton Literary Series. She is also a poet (*Listen to the Green, Postcard from the Shore,* and other volumes), and she has recently turned to prose (*God in the Dark.*) "The Muse Is Much Amused" is her first attempt at fiction. "What is meta*phor?*" has been one of the burning issues in her life.

ROBERT SIEGEL is a poet whose books include *In a Pig's Eye* and *The Beasts & The Elders* as well as the fiction *Whalesong* and *Alpha Centauri.* He is professor of English at the University of Wisconsin—Milwaukee and has taught at Dartmouth, Wheaton, Princeton, and Goethe University in Frankfurt.

WALTER WANGERIN, JR. , a former pastor of Grace Lutheran Church in Evansville, Indiana, now devotes full time to his writing. He is happily remembered for such fiction as *Miz Lil and the Chronicles of Grace* and *The Book of the Dun Cow,* and for such children's books as *Potter* and *In the Beginning There Was No Sky.*